DRAGON LORD

DRAGONS & PHOENIXES BOOK ONE

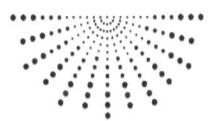

MIRANDA MARTIN

NADIA HUNTER

BLURB

The world outside the cities went to hell a long time ago. When pollution got so bad it burned away the ozone layer, humans built protective domes in order to survive. Now, between the radiated air and the fighting among dragons and phoenixes, it's not safe to go outside.

I'm a transporter. Self employed in a dangerous world, delivering valuable goods from client to recipient. But I never take on the more lucrative dome to dome jobs.

When someone breaks into my apartment looking to hire me, I refuse flat out. One, I don't like being forced. Two, the job requires leaving the dome. Three, the package is a sun-sick kid. Half-human, half-phoenix and I'm supposed to take him back to his phoenix family. Oh hell no!

But the client reveals he knows my secret, blackmailing me into a job I don't want with stakes that grow higher each day.

I have to take the kid straight through the Dragon Lord's territory. Everyone knows that's suicide. Coming face to face with the dominant, sexy Dragon Lord reveals the truth about my heritage and puts me in more danger than I knew existed.

CHAPTER ONE

*T*his was the address, according to my watch.

The large warehouse didn't look like anything special from where I stood in the shadows, in an alley across a narrow street. The building was one in a line of many, all in various states of disrepair. The synthetic wood paneling had been painted at some point, but it was so discolored and had peeled so much that I could only guess at what the original color was. A flicker of movement in the hazy window of a nearby building caught my eye and I glanced over. A reflexive sign of nervousness I couldn't stop.

Nothing. But that didn't mean nobody was there.

Every part of the city dome was crowded, but bad areas like this one gave the appearance of being sparsely or not-at-all populated. However, that wasn't because people weren't here. It was because those who lived and survived in places like this knew better than to make themselves known. A person in plain sight was a potential target. When I had to be seen, I made an effort to appear strong—eyes forward, confident stride. I was already at a disadvantage being a young woman.

Every so often, developers tried to come in and clean the place up. Space was at a premium since expansion was limited. They never got far. The residents here made sure of it.

I looked up and down the street, scanning the few older vehicles parked on the side. Most of them had already gathered a thick layer of dust. At closer inspection, key components of each of them were stripped. Lovely. I doubted any of them were even functional.

Good thing I didn't bring my car. With traffic the way it was, and the maze of narrow streets that were closed down for repairs that never happened, it didn't make sense for me to drive much. I rarely took my old piece of junk on a job unless the package I needed to deliver was heavy or bulky.

I was much faster on foot. Speed was more important to me than the dubious convenience of a car. On the other hand, not having an enclosed vehicle also meant that I had to be on my toes. There was no metal and glass between me and everyone out here.

I adjusted my grip on the slick handle of the briefcase I held down at my side, considering the deceptive emptiness of the street.

Ah, the joys of self-employment. Sometimes I had to remind myself why I got into certain situations.

Times like this.

I started my carrier service, Mia Hill Delivery, a few years ago after I found myself without a job. With so little employment opportunities and so many people willing to work for non-living wages, job stability was a joke in most sectors. Going out on my own and building my own business was a difficult decision, though it ultimately paid off.

I'm glad I did it. I might not make a lot, but I had enough to get by and I didn't have to answer to anyone but myself. Suited me just fine.

There were definite pitfalls, though.

The main con was that I often had to go into the shadier areas of the dome. I knew I couldn't compete with the larger services that only took jobs with limited liability. Deliveries that were completely clean and on the up-and-up with the so-called respectable sections of society.

So I targeted the somewhat less respectable. They were underserved. For good reason, but a market was a market. I was hungry enough to make it work. I built my reputation on being discreet, fast, and reliable.

The fact that I was a company of one also helped. The paranoid thought there was less of a chance of something going wrong if there was only one person involved. They might also have thought I'd be easier to lean on or control, but if it got me work, they could believe what they wanted. So long as I was paid on time for my services, of course.

It was times like this, when I found myself hanging out in a dark alley lined with trash and intermittent shallow pools of mysterious liquid that stuck to the soles of my boots that I wondered if it was time to bring someone else on.

If something seemed a little more dangerous than I could handle, I might tell my neighbor Jacob where I was going, just in case. But I tried not to do that before I left, because then he tried to insist on going with me. I had given in a couple of times, and both times his presence had only escalated the situation.

Guys saw him and wanted to prove they could take him. They were wrong but I didn't particularly want to get into a fight every time I went on a job. As it was, if anything went south in this part of the city dome, I was on my own.

It was a well-known fact that cops only showed up in the nice neighborhoods. Where the rich greased their palms, essentially converting public law enforcement into a private security detail. Corruption. Wasn't it grand?

I looked at my watch again. One minute left.

Showtime.

I stepped out of the alley, my boots silent against the asphalt as I crossed the empty road. The spot between my shoulders itched from the idea of multiple pairs of eyes on me. More than a few of the broken, dingy windows that looked out onto the road were likely occupied with people curious to see what I was doing. And wondering if they could get something out of it, no doubt.

I forced myself to keep my head straight, only using my peripheral vision to keep an eye around me. If I acted like a mark, I was much more likely to be jumped. I touched one of my knives, the smooth hilt calming my tightly controlled nerves.

The door to the warehouse was rusted and old, but it didn't budge when I pounded on it. Reinforced. It looked old, but that was likely deliberate. It was window dressing, added on by whoever took control of the place. One more thing to show me that nothing here could be trusted.

I didn't have to wait long for a response. The door opened smoothly, with no eerie creaking sound like its appearance might have suggested.

I blinked at the overly developed chest that was suddenly at my eye level. Two odd bumps around the nipple area suggested he was into piercings. I tilted my head back and looked up at the man with the thick neck. Sunlight coming through the filter of the dome glinted off his bald head. His eyes were small and close together, his nose slightly off center from being broken, most likely more than once. His jaw was heavy and clean-shaven. His black t-shirt was tight enough to show off the very large muscles of his shoulders and arms, with black trousers and boots adding to his mono-chromatic look.

He had a couple of shiny knives in holsters on either side

of his hips, but I knew just from looking at them that they didn't get much use. I glanced at his hands, taking in the calluses and the scarred knuckles. The knives were just for show. This guy used his fists. I might have been more intimidated if I wasn't preoccupied thinking about his nipple piercings. Was he a simple bar or hoop guy? Or were they sparkly?

Important questions.

"Delivery," I finally offered when he just stared at me.

He nodded, stepping back and gesturing into the dim interior. Why, yes, large scary man. I'd be more than happy to step into your isolated, dark warehouse. That seems like an excellent idea.

I stepped inside anyway.

The hair on the back of my neck stood straight up. I didn't have a great feeling about this but I'd never left a job uncompleted before and I wasn't going to start now. I had a reputation to maintain. Such as it was.

Inside, the cavernous space was lit by a few spaced-out bulbs hanging from a high ceiling. Crates were stacked in massive columns and rows. There was only one path to take, and crates lined both sides of it.

"This way," he said in surprisingly high-pitched voice for a man so massive. I wondered if he got so built just to preempt any jokes about it.

I followed behind his bulky frame, my eyes peeled for anyone else. If there were more people hidden among the crates, they were deliberately still and quiet.

The path twisted and turned, with multiple places where there was more than one direction you could go. As he led me through, I made sure to memorize the path we took. I could see why they had the crates in here arranged this way. It would be hard to break in and find what you were looking for and it would be difficult to leave if they didn't want you to.

It would be so easy to get lost. What a comforting thought. I repeated the turns in my head.

We walked for a full two minutes before the narrow walkway through the crates ended abruptly, and we came out into a clear space.

It wasn't what I expected. It looked like an average office. Well, except for the fact that it was in the middle of a dim warehouse. There was a desk set in the center with a cushioned chair behind it. There were no chairs in front for guests. Guess they didn't have many of those. Or at least not ones they wanted to be comfortable.

Filing cabinets in an industrial-beige color defined the sides of the square area. I wondered if there was actual paper in them. It was difficult to come by. As with most things, a synthetic material was available, but it was expensive. There was even a bookshelf directly behind the desk, though I couldn't read the spines of the books from this far away. They looked old and worn, as most books did these days. Digital was the norm. It didn't need physical space and paper was, as I said, expensive.

Whoever had designed this place had an old-school office in mind. I was guessing it was the middle-aged man sitting behind the desk.

He was small, balding, and dressed in a tightly fitted pinstriped suit. Unfortunate. It showed off his narrow shoulders and his small belly, the kind that grew when you had a desk job. His face was round, his cheeks full, and small wire-rimmed glasses sat on his equally round nose. He smiled at me, but it didn't reach his eyes. He might have looked like a mid-level executive, but the mild exterior was meaningless.

"You have a delivery for me?" he asked pleasantly enough, his eyes glancing over at the briefcase I still had attached to my wrist.

"Yes." I looked up at the other two guards he had waiting

on either side of him, a few steps back, their outfits and demeanor the same as the guy who brought me in here. They gave me hard stares, ready to tackle me if I made the wrong move. I was not moving forward until I got an invitation.

"Bring it here," the man ordered.

A please would have been nice, but that was probably asking a little too much.

I nodded and stepped forward. Using my fingerprint, I undid the custom handcuffs that attached the briefcase to my wrist. It had been a splurge to get something so secure, but it had been worth it. If I used the wrong finger, it would be locked for twenty-four hours.

I also had the option of setting it to detonate if it sensed my vitals declining—either because someone killed me or because they chopped off my hand. Gruesome, but it would be a good deterrent. Not that I ever activated that feature. But any would be thieves wouldn't know that.

Pocketing the handcuffs, I set the briefcase down carefully on the desk. I had no idea what was in it and that's the way I liked to keep it. All I asked was if the contents were fragile. In this case, they weren't.

The man reached out with his small, well-manicured hands, the gold watch on his wrist glimmering even in this lighting. Gaudy. But I guess it matched the stark pinstripe of his suit. He'd probably watched one too many classic mob movies. He pulled the briefcase over to his side of the desk and opened it. I still couldn't make out what was in it as he scanned the content with his eyes.

"Looks like it's all here," he murmured, closing the briefcase again and smiling at me. "Thank you for your services."

"Of course." Now, to get out of here. I really hoped this would be easy. I took a step back from the desk and sensed movement behind me. I didn't take my eyes off the guy in charge. "I'll just be leaving now," I said in an even voice. Maybe being confident and saying it out loud would help.

A girl could dream. Even before he replied, I knew shit was going to hit the fan.

"I'm afraid I can't let you do that," he replied just as evenly. "You see, we just can't have anyone walking around with knowledge of this." He smiled slightly. "And I promised Benny to take care of you in exchange for what you have so thoughtfully delivered."

I had an urge to ask knowledge of what, since I still had no idea what was in the briefcase, but I knew it didn't matter. He'd already decided to kill me.

And he'd get away with it.

Benny, the dick-hole who hired me, was so going to regret this. Assuming I got out of here.

If I died, there really wasn't anyone who would notice apart from my landlord when rent didn't arrive and my neighbor Jacob. I might not have told Jacob where I was going before I left, but I did leave a note about it on my kitchen counter in case something happened to me. I'd probably be dead by the time he went into my apartment looking for me, but at least he'd know what happened. I also told him in the note not to come after me.

Jacob had a pretty sketchy past that he wasn't all that open with. From what I could glean, he'd spent quite a bit of time as a mercenary outside the city domes. He might decide to come and find out in person any way. And then he might be hurt. Maybe addresses weren't a good thing to leave for him to find. On the other hand, he could find out where I'd gone by hacking into the computer in my office, which I knew he could do. He had quite a list of skills for a baker.

All of that ran through my head as I pulled my knives out of their holsters. At the very least, I'd make sure I did some damage.

The security on either side of the desk started walking towards me even as I stepped to the side to keep an eye on the guy behind me as well. Taking on all three of them was stupid. If any one of them got their hands on me, they could probably break me in half with all their steroid-enhanced muscles. No, I needed to get through the first guy and run.

But I needed to move fast, before they got any closer.

All in.

Turning to the guy who initially opened the door, I sprinted straight at him. His eyes widened at the unexpected move, though he kept his position.

As I drew close, he reached out to grab me but I ducked and used both knives to slice at the backs of his legs, aiming for his tendons. Incapacitating him.

He shouted as I dodged around him and shoved him forward, towards the other two who had picked up speed. My heart was pounding hard enough it was hitting my chest wall. There was a metallic taste in my mouth as adrenaline rushed through my veins.

Right, left, straight. I tried to remember the exact directions to reach the door, hoping I hadn't forgotten one. A dead end at this point would actually mean death for me. How appropriate.

Crashes sounded from behind as the men's large bodies hit the crates. People that heavy and large just weren't fast. The narrowness of the passageway was in my favor. Being smaller, I didn't crash into anything even at breakneck speed.

If I made it out of here, I was going to kill Benny, the little weasel who hired me for this job. My guess was that he knew exactly how this would go down. No wonder didn't negotiate with me when I named my price. He never expected to have to pay the second half.

I knew I shouldn't have taken the job. He'd given off bad vibes, but I needed the money.

The lit edge of the door leading out finally came into view and a renewed burst of energy suffused my screaming leg muscles.

I might have actually made it, but then another large shape stepped in front of the door. Where did these guys come from?

I didn't slow down, the men running after me were too close, and I couldn't stop my momentum. They were breathing hard. From the sounds, cardio wasn't a priority for them. Probably the intimidating look of their muscles was more than enough in most cases.

I turned the knives in my hands as I ran and locked my eyes on the new guy's body. This really wasn't the ideal way to do this. It would be so embarrassing if I fell and impaled myself on my own knives.

I pulled my arm back and held my breath for a few strides.

Steady...

Wait...

I launched the knife, aiming at his torso, and watched it fly end over end. I didn't really want to kill the guy, but aiming for something like his leg would be idiotic. And he knew what he signed up for when he took this job. Also, I seriously doubted he would lose any sleep over killing me.

He shifted to the side as he saw the knife coming, but it flew too fast. It pierced his side with a meaty thud, the hilt sticking out.

"Bitch!" he cried out, his hand going to the knife hilt along with all his attention.

Not very well trained. I took advantage of his distraction.

As I reached him, I lifted my leg up and kicked the exposed hilt of my knife through his clutching hands, shoving the blade deeper into his side. He screamed, stumbling as I shoved him away from the door.

"Fair enough," I threw out over my shoulder as my hands undid the lock on the door and I shoved it open. I was lucky it was an old-fashioned one and not one of those that required a password or a fingerprint.

Small favors.

I stumbled out into the light as the stabbed guy let out a string of curses behind me, shooting straight out across the road and into the alley that I'd come from. I needed to get to the closest area with dense traffic. Luckily, I was paranoid enough that I planned out an escape route beforehand for every job I took. If I went a few blocks east, I'd hit one of the busiest streets in this area.

There was no way those goons were going to catch me on foot. They were already on their last legs, judging from how hard they were gasping after such a short distance.

This was why I made sure to get my run in every morning. Being fast and having stamina could mean the difference between getting away or being caught by a nipple-ringed body builder with a high voice. I could outrun most people, but it was nice that these guys were so slow. I couldn't always depend on the thugs chasing me to be so muscle-bound and so against aerobic activity.

Maybe I'd send them a jazzercise e-chip as a thank you.

There were still footsteps behind me, but they were getting further and further away now that I had more room and could run flat out. The alleyway gave way to a narrow street with liquor stores and pawnshops on either side. Not the best street, but better than the warehouse district.

I ducked into another narrow alley, this one so narrow that I had to turn sideways so I could scoot through. No way could any of those guys do that. Their man boobs weren't nearly as malleable as mine. Though they might have been bigger. And even I didn't get out of there without a few scrapes.

The alley spit me out into a river of humanity, people irritably crammed in together as they tried to reach their destinations as quickly as possible. It was lunchtime, which meant it was more crowded than it would have been otherwise.

Perfect.

I slowed down, catching my breath as I stepped into the crowd and began walking at the same pace. Running through this throng of moving bodies would be a dead giveaway if someone was watching. One of the reasons I didn't use a motorcycle was how visible it would make me when most people walked. It would have also limited my choices since only select roads allowed motor traffic.

I let the crowd carry me a few blocks down, keeping an eye out for the guys who were after me.

Nothing.

Once I was sure I'd shaken my pursuers, I peeled away to the other side of the road and broke into a jog. Anger had me gritting my teeth and turning away from the street that would take me back to my place.

No. I had somewhere else to go first.

I stuck to the more-crowded streets as I made my way over to the nicely-kept buildings in the prosperous part of this section. They were mostly residences, with a few convenience stores on the first floors. I rode one of the automated trolleys to cut the distance in half.

It wasn't near my place or my office. But I didn't care. I was angry enough to traverse the length of the whole dome if I had to.

I hopped off the trolley and walked the last block to the narrow stone building that was my destination. Fake trees lined the street. It wasn't worth the resources to plant real ones even in this posh area.

I tested the gleaming door, polished within an inch of its

life, but it was locked with a retina scanner. I wasn't getting in this way. At least not without my tools and some study. Luckily, most upper-story windows weren't very secure.

I walked to the side of the building and found the fire escape but it was a ways off the ground.

Hmm.

Slipping into the space between that building and the one next to it, I took a running start and jumped to bounce off the neighboring building and reach for the fire escape.

My palms slammed into the cool metal.

Ouch. A ninja I was not. But at least I made it.

Cursing, I climbed up the fire escape and started counting off the floors.

Whenever I got a new client, I followed them home to make sure their address was accurate—at a discreet distance of course. Didn't want to lose business. But I'd been burned before when someone didn't want to pay and their address had been fake. If the two didn't match up, I didn't take the case.

As it was, I knew exactly where Benny lived. That rat assumed I'd be dead after all. What did it matter if I knew his address? And look—his window was conveniently located right next to the fire escape.

I leaned over to peer inside. Not seeing anyone at first glance, I wondered if I was going to have to wait until after work was over for him to get home, but then I spotted Benny sitting on a couch in the living room, a cup of something hot in his hands. Must be nice to not have to hustle like the rest of us.

I reached into my pocket and pulled out one of the tiny devices that I made sure to always have on my person. I suctioned it to the glass and pushed the little blinking button that indicated it was activated. It tapped the glass just hard enough to create a network of hairline cracks. I carefully took it off the glass and slid it back into my jacket pocket. I'd bought the oversized army green thing because it had so many pockets. A purse didn't really fit with my lifestyle.

Holding on to the railing, I leaned out and kicked through the window. I didn't have to use much force at all. My boots and the thick fabric of my jeans protected my leg from the sharp pieces. A cry came from inside the apartment as I used my boot to sweep away some of the glass from the sill before I stepped inside, careful not to touch the shards.

"What are you doing here? Get out right now or I'll call the police!"

"Go ahead and call them," I said calmly. "I'll wait."

I watched his eyes move over to the communications panel but he didn't take a step towards it. Both he and I knew he wasn't calling the cops. That would draw attention to him that he didn't want.

Sure, the cops were bribed. But if Benny was a threat to any of the other loaded residents in this area, they'd bring him down. Couldn't have the criminal element living here, after all. Which was a joke in and of itself considering how a lot of the rich made their money.

I took a step towards him, taking in the leopard print robe he was wearing. That thing was offensively ugly. And I had a sneaking suspicion he wasn't wearing anything underneath it.

Eww.

"I'm here for the second half of my payment. Plus hazard pay," I added, my eyes boring into him.

"Couldn't you just send me a bill!" he exclaimed, edging towards the door.

I shook my head and stepped in front of it.

He stopped, his narrow throat moving as he swallowed.

"No, I couldn't," I said, crossing my arms. I made sure he had a nice view of my remaining dagger.

His eyes moved towards it, his hand coming up to push back his dark curls. They were so shiny and full of product I was surprised they moved at all.

"Okay, fine." He smoothed down his robe and moved over to the com panel, which he would have to use to pay me. "How much do I owe you?"

"Triple."

"Triple!" he cried out, his voice incredulous. "I'm not going to pay you triple!"

I deliberately pulled out my dagger, tapping it against my palm.

"You sent me there to die. You said it was a simple drop off. You're lucky all I'm asking for is triple," I said softly.

He eyes slid away.

Guilty.

"If something happened, it's not my fault," he muttered.

"He told me you had a deal. That in exchange for whatever I delivered, he would take care of me for you."

His lips tightened. He was caught and he knew it.

"That rat," Benny muttered under his breath. Rich coming from him. "Look I don't know what he told you—"

"Triple. Or I take my payment in a much less comfortable way for you."

I twirled my knife, the sharp edge catching the light. I didn't plan on actually hurting him but he didn't know that.

"Now you're just being unreasonable –"

He let out a yelp as I threw the knife. He didn't have to know it was my last one. The hilt vibrated as it stuck out from the wall, a foot to the side of his head.

"Okay! Okay!" he blabbered, his hands up in the air. "I'll give you what you want!"

He was cooperative enough after that.

After I used my watch to make sure the funds were transferred to my account, I opened the front door.

"Oh, and I'm not available for you to hire again," I said over my shoulder.

"Yeah. Sure," he scoffed, shaking his head. "You won't find me in a ten-mile radius of the hellhole you work in."

I nodded. "Good. If I have any more trouble, I know exactly where to come to find you. You should probably let your friend know that this particular deal is off."

He sputtered, but I closed the door behind myself and stepped out into the hall before he could say anything else.

Maybe I should've asked for quadruple.

CHAPTER TWO

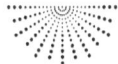

*I*t was still only afternoon when I headed back to my office. With how much had happened, it seemed like it should have been a week later. I needed a nap. I kept my eyes open on the way, just in case, but I was fairly certain that I was fine for now. Still, I felt a little safer as I merged with the crowd again.

Tilting my head back, I looked up at the dome as I let the stream of people carry me forward. The harsh rays of the sun were dialed down to a gentle illumination as they passed through the protective barrier. The large, hexagonal sections showcased the clear blue sky outside, the searing sun the only break in it. Someone bumped into me and I looked back down.

"Hey! Watch where you're going!" the bearded man yelled at me over his shoulder as he barreled past. Par for the course.

I passed through the biggest open market in this quadrant of the dome on my way to the office, so I stopped at a stall to pick out lunch. Lifting my wrist to the sensor, I paid for the food, transferring funds through my watch. I thanked the small man behind the register as he handed me a warm, wrapped package. The smell of garlic and freshly baked bread wafted out. My mouth watered. My stomach growled like it had been years since I'd eaten.

I stepped back onto the walkway and headed down the street while the different stall owners called out their wares.

"Synthetic fish! Just like the real thing!"

I really hoped it wasn't. That stuff tasted like crap.

"Feeling lonely? Need a release? The best virtual reality experience in the dome is right here!"

I glanced over at the enclosed stall and shuddered. I wouldn't want to touch anything in there with a ten-foot pole.

"Want to head out of the dome? You're going to need masks and protective clothes!"

I wouldn't buy that stuff from here. It could be counterfeit. And the guy would run off before you could come back to him with burns and breathing issues due to the faulty equipment.

It was possible I was in a cynical mood.

Any time, day or night, the market was open with almost anything you could want on display. Not that I ever had the urge to buy glow-in-the-dark underwear or tambourines at one in the morning. But it was nice to know the option was there.

I pushed through the rush of the market and out into the street that my office was on. It wasn't the best street but neither was it the worst. I deliberately found something that was in the middle so it wouldn't alienate anyone right off the bat.

Probably I should check to see if anything looked suspicious before I went in. The guys chasing me might have decided I was worth the extra effort. I crossed the street and walked by the building once to make sure that no nasty surprises were waiting. The gray brick structure with the short stoop looked just like it had when I'd left. The dentist on one side and the consignment shop on the other looked the same as well. I wouldn't know if someone was waiting for me unless I went inside.

Mentally shrugging, I crossed the street and hopped up the steps. Might as well face the issue head on.

The door at the top of the short flight of stairs didn't actually lead to the office, but to the foyer. Generic flooring and lighting greeted anyone who entered, along with an equally bland staircase that led to other businesses who leased space here. I turned to the left of the staircase where the door to my office was situated.

The frosted glass with my name in gold lettering greeted me as I opened the door. The actual office wasn't much to see. I had one room that I furnished with a worn desk, a wheeled chair for me, and two chairs for potential clients. The cabinets that I had against one wall housed all of the things that I might need during a job. Handcuffs, different kinds of clothing, makeup, and so on. Not that I used the makeup or fancier clothes much. But from time to time, I had to make a delivery at a social event. Going in the way I usually dressed would make me stand out too much. I had one sad-looking painting of what I thought might have been a bird on the wall opposite my desk. And that was about as far as I could go with décor. Anyway. It all looked like I'd left it.

Except for the stranger waiting in one of the client chairs.

I paused in the doorway. I'd just used a retinal scanner to enter. The door locked automatically when I left the office. How did this guy get in?

He looked over at me with cool gray eyes. His suit was made of a tasteful, dark gray material, obviously custom fit to his narrow frame. His lightly lined face was handsome in an uninteresting way, his hair a bright shock of white above it. The scarlet red of his tie was the only color in his whole outfit.

"How did you get in here?" I demanded, my hand going for my knife. I'd made sure to pull it out of the wall after I'd thrown it at Benny. I didn't want to lose both of my favorite knives in one day.

The man raised his eyebrows as my hand closed over the hilt, but he didn't look worried.

"Retinal scanners aren't foolproof. You know that," he admonished quietly. "I'm sorry if I frightened you." His tone said he wasn't at all sorry. "I wouldn't have come in if I'd known when you were coming back. As it was, I didn't want to have to wait in the hall for who knew how long."

He was right about the retinal scanners. I knew from personal experience, but always from the other side. It wasn't comfortable at all to experience it from the perspective of the person whose property had been broken into.

"What do you want?" I asked. My instinct was to say no from the get go. But someone this persistent likely wouldn't accept the no without at least being heard first.

"Well, to hire you, of course."

I gave him a level stare, calculating the danger he posed. The stranger was already in my office but he hadn't attacked me yet. He had a good amount of money, judging from that suit. It wouldn't hurt to give him a moment to say his piece.

"Fine." I walked around him to sit down on the plush chair on the other side of the desk, trying not to show how laser-focused I was on him the entire time. "If you give me the details of the job, I'll let you know whether or not I'm willing to take it."

He raised his surprisingly dark eyebrows again and leaned forward. "Oh, I think you'll want to take this one. It will pay very handsomely. Very handsomely indeed."

Money was important. I couldn't take it for granted after I'd spent years trying to make ends meet but I still needed to avoid making stupid decisions about the jobs I took. The money sometimes just wasn't worth it.

"What's your name?" I probed, leaning back in my chair.

"Santiago," he supplied readily.

No first name.

"Mr. Santiago, you tell me what the job is, and I'll tell you whether or not I want to take it," I repeated.

"I understand, Ms. Hill. I need a package delivered immediately."

I nodded, opening a drawer and pulling out my tablet and stylus. The technology was old, but I always thought better with my hand in motion. "I can do that, assuming all my requirements are met. What is the delivery timeframe? And what is the destination?" I waited with my stylus poised above the screen.

"The timeframe is as soon as possible, within the week if you can. And the destination is the nearest phoenix territory."

I set my stylus down with a hard click.

I'd never been outside the dome, at least not past the safe zone buffer set up around it. I promised my mother never to venture any farther than that. And I had no intention of ever breaking that promise.

"I'm sorry. I have a firm policy against taking jobs outside the dome." I stood smiling stiffly. "I'm sorry I couldn't help you today. I could recommend a few other agencies that have good reputations, if you would like."

Santiago made no move to stand. "I must insist that you take the job," he said, his eyes calm and steady.

"And I repeat, I do not take jobs that take me out of the dome," I repeated slowly. "Now, if you wouldn't like the names of some other agencies, I would appreciate it if you left me to my work."

He still made no move to stand. Was I going to have to physically throw an old man out of my office?

"You know, it's very interesting how much you can find out of about a person simply by watching them for a week or two," he said.

This wasn't going anywhere good. I narrowed my eyes at him. "I'm in no mood for games," I warned.

"Oh, my dear, this is no game, I assure you." He shook his head, interlocking his fingers over one knee. "But wouldn't you find it curious if someone were to, say, leave the dome twice a week at the same time every week? Not to go anywhere. Simply to sit in the safe zone for an hour or so."

My stomach dropped a little. "Get out."

My voice was low. I was not trying to be polite anymore.

"Now, now. Let's not be hasty." He deliberately crossed his legs and made no move to stand once again. "Now, if someone were to find out such a fact out about another, I personally would find it very suspicious. After all, what need would a full human have to stand out in direct sunlight? Why, it would cause severe burns without the right protection! And her lungs wouldn't fare too well either without a proper mask to protect against the air." His unblinking stare watched me, like a predator eyeing its prey.

"What do you want?" I finally gritted out through my teeth.

This was a threat, plain and simple. One that he was using to force me into doing his bidding. Otherwise, he would have already reported me to the authorities.

He smiled gently. "It's straightforward. Simply deliver this package to its destination, and no one need know about your peculiar habits. Everyone is allowed their foibles after all." He finally decided to stand up. "You'll find my card in your inbox. Think it over. Though I would caution you against refusing. People have been banished—or worse—for far less."

I watched as he stepped towards the door, opened it with a glance over his shoulder at me, and then closed it just as quietly.

I tapped the screen of my watch to find the card. Just his name and a phone number. Still no first name. Just Santiago.

I slowly sank back down onto my seat. Any which way I looked at this, I was screwed.

Some days, it just didn't pay to get out of bed.

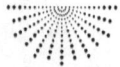

CHAPTER THREE

I sat at my desk and just stared at the number for a while.

I should've been more careful when I left the dome. Years of nothing going wrong had made me complacent. Complacent and stupid. But that was something I couldn't go back and undo. I could only be more careful moving forward, if I survived this job. I shook my head, leaning back in my chair and covering my face with my hands.

When I used to ask my mother about my father, she would tell me that he wasn't someone that I should seek out. That it wasn't safe for me to be outside the city dome. That I needed to stay inside where humans made certain that neither dragons nor phoenixes could enter. She would answer me in such a stern and final manner that I learned not to ask too many questions for fear of angering or upsetting her.

Twice a week, every week, we would leave the city dome briefly to go out into the sun and take the necessary dose of its direct light. Just enough to be healthy, but not an excessive amount.

She drilled into me that I needed to be careful. It wasn't safe for me to be anything else, so I needed to give every appearance of being fully human. We never spoke about it. The only connection I had to the other part of my nature was the trips outside the dome. Maybe I would have pushed the issue, asked for more information when I was older.

But I didn't get the chance.

When I was twelve, she was diagnosed with a particularly virulent type of breast cancer. She was gone within a few months. I never got the chance to probe her for more answers.

Even on her deathbed, she made sure to make me promise that I would never leave the dome. I remember her pale face, her shallow breathing, how much weight she'd lost fighting the inevitable. Her grip had been surprisingly tight, her eyes intense as she'd told me to stay in the dome after she was gone, to never leave its safety.

"I love you more than anything. You must stay safe here," she'd said as she'd relaxed back onto the bed.

Not long after that, she was gone forever. It left me empty inside. I couldn't imagine my life without her, her steady, strong presence and the surety of her love.

Life continued even when it felt like it shouldn't.

As soon as she died, the authorities took me in. The foster home that I stayed in for the next six years of my life was okay. They weren't abusive but they were simply doing it for the money. As soon as I was eighteen and legal, I left and found a tiny room to call my own.

The winding road since had landed me here.

I stared at the numbers some more.

Even as I sat and turned over the possibilities, I knew there was no real choice. If I didn't take the job and Santiago exposed me, I would be banished from the dome at the very least. At worst, I might be executed. Maybe not by the authorities, but by panicked humans.

They thought dragons and phoenixes were to be dealt with at a distance.

A safe distance.

The war had really stoked anti-dragon and anti-phoenix sentiment and the ensuing years of separation had only cemented it. If the people here found out...

Knowing that I was here among them would not go over well. I would lose everything I'd worked so hard to build. And I would end up outside the dome anyway. At least if I took the job, there was a chance to avoid that outcome.

No, there really was no choice. I was just delaying the inevitable. I really hated having my hand forced.

As night fell, I walked home to my apartment. I'd had the option of working from home and cutting my overhead, but I knew I'd end up regretting cutting that particular corner with the kinds of people who often found their way to me.

I kept my home address private.

Taking the stairs two at a time, I walked down the some-what dingy hallway and stopped at my door. The retinal scanner and fingerprint lock had been installed by me. This place only came with physical locks, but I would rather have all three.

The inside of my apartment was spare. There wasn't a lot of room and I wasn't fussy.

Okay, no more delaying. I sat down on my comfortable, broken-in sofa and dialed the number. It only rang twice before he picked up.

"Santiago."

"I'll take it. I'll take the job. But if you try to strong-arm me ever again, you'll regret it."

"You are in no position to threaten," he countered mildly. "I'm sending an address. Be there at seven o'clock in the morning. I'm transferring funds to your account for anything you might need for the trip along with half the payment. You'll receive the second half after the job is completed."

He ended the phone call, not waiting for a response.

Charming.

Curious, I accessed my account to see how much he'd sent over. I blinked at the amount. Wow. This was half the amount? At least the job was lucrative.

I took a deep breath, stood up, and pulled out my bag to start packing. It wouldn't take me long. My cramped studio didn't hold much, and I wasn't one to buy a lot of unnecessary clothes anyway. I was packed in twenty minutes flat. I still needed to go get supplies for the trip though. Pulling my boots back on, I left my apartment and climbed down the stairs.

Outside, the street was still bustling even though it was so late. Breaking into a jog, I caught one of the trolleys as it went by, hopping up with a grip on one of the cool metal poles on the side. It didn't take me long to reach the marketplace.

I went straight to Maryam's stall.

"Hey, Mia. What do you need?" she asked as she packed something up for someone else.

"Rations for three weeks," I said, looking over the survival gear she had stocked in her large stall. I needed food that was compact and light and that wouldn't spoil quickly in the heat. I trusted Maryam to know what I needed. Unlike some of the more transient vendors here, Maryam had been in this same spot for years. I usually just came to her for the occasional knife or holster, which she also carried.

She raised her brows at me, rubbing the side of her shaven head. The movement threw her muscled arms into sharp relief, highlighting the scorpion tattoo on her bicep.

"Three weeks? Do you need water containers to along with that?"

"Yes."

"All right, I can help you with that. Are you leaving the dome?" she asked as she got started pulling things.

It was a fair question. There would be no other reason for me to need three weeks of rations. The city dome was big but it wasn't that big. And I'd be able to buy food at every corner.

"Yes," I confirmed and left it at that. The fewer people who knew about this job, the better. If I finished it with my life intact, I didn't want word to get around that I took these kinds of jobs. It would attract the kind of clientele I didn't want.

"Someone finally paid enough to get you out of here?" she asked with a grin. "It's dangerous out there, that's for sure. But I'm told the money is good."

"Yeah. It's good for a reason," I point out. "But this is a special circumstance," I added firmly.

"Copy that," she said easily. "Here are the rations," she said handing me the tough canvas bag. "If you bring your vehicle around when you're leaving, I can load up the water directly into it. It'll be too heavy for you to carry back."

"Sounds good. I'll swing by in the morning."

"I'll be here."

I gave her a sloppy salute and shouldered the bag, fighting through the crowd to return back home.

Truth be told, I didn't know how well my car was going to fare out there. It wasn't built for leaving the dome, at least not for a human. I wondered how I was going to explain that away if anyone asked. It wasn't like I had another car to fall back on.

Clothing and food taken care of, when I got back to my apartment, I got to work organizing and packing my weapons. Two bows, one specialized for shorter distances and one for longer distances. They were the best defense humans had against both dragons and phoenixes since they couldn't make gunpowder anymore, being confined to the domes with no way to gather resources.

Next came the various knives. And the sword Jacob had given me for my birthday last year. I wasn't the best with a sword, but Jacob's training had brought me up to competent. I figured it was probably best to take everything I had. I didn't know what to expect.

I stared at everything I'd laid out on the floor.

I needed to tell Jacob. I wasn't looking forward to this conversation. But I was packed and this was the only time I'd have to do it. I left my apartment and went to the one right next to it. Jacob's security was even more hardcore than mine. Made me feel a little less paranoid about my setup.

When he first moved in here a few years ago, I expected to treat him just like I treated everybody else. Say hello if I saw him and that was about it. But Jacob wasn't the kind of guy who would be kept at a distance when he didn't want to be.

He'd seen me at the practice range with my bow and had walked right on over even though I was exuding my best stay away vibes. He'd asked about my bow and shown me his. And when I'd said I wasn't interested in dating him, he'd just laughed.

"I wouldn't want to date anyone as good with a bow as you are," he'd said, his grin inviting me to enjoy the joke with him. "I'm not always the best boyfriend. And I have a true aversion to being shot."

I'd laughed despite myself. And he'd gotten it in his head that we needed to be friends. So he started showing up with beers and that smile.

Eventually he started opening up about himself, about the bakery he decided to open in his old age—which was a crock because he was only a couple of years older than me. He appeared so open about himself that I hadn't realized exactly how closed off he was about his past until I'd inadvertently asked him a question about it. He'd glossed over it, easily changing the subject.

From what I'd gleaned over the time I knew him, he'd been a mercenary for years before deciding to go full civilian. As a baker, no less. With his muscled build, dark hair buzzed short against his skull, and a scar running down the side of his interesting face, he wasn't the kind of guy you would expect to be baking cupcakes at four in the morning. But that was exactly who he was.

I wasn't above admitting to the fact that his brownies were what finally sold me on him. I could be friends if he kept feeding my addiction for those little pieces of chocolate heaven. Before I knew it, I spent more time with him than anyone else.

So. I needed to talk to him or I'd feel like a dick. I knocked on his door. I didn't usually bother him so late because he was always up so early to open his place for morning customers, but I knew he'd be beyond mad if I didn't tell him this in person. I'd briefly considered writing him a note, but then decided I wasn't quite that big a chicken.

I smiled a little as faint cursing came through the door, staying in full view of his security camera so he'd know it was me. The sound of the door unlocking came next. It swung open and he looked out at me slightly bleary-eyed, his t-shirt and pajama pants letting me know he'd literally stumbled out of bed. His face, a pretty blend of multiple races that I couldn't ever quite pinpoint, was creased on one side from the pillow. His brown torso carried more than a few scars, but I was sure the marks only helped with the ladies.

Not that I ever saw any over at his place. I was assuming

he went over to theirs, considering how much of a security freak he was.

"Mia?" he asked, his eyes clearing as he automatically glanced down both sides of the hall. "Is something wrong?"

I took a deep breath and let it out. Straight to the point. "I got a job. I'm leaving the dome for a few weeks tomorrow." If all went well, it would be two or less. But I wanted to give myself more time because who knew if it would be a smooth journey.

He blinked at me. "What?"

Before I could explain myself, he snagged my forearm and pulled me inside, shutting the door. "You're leaving the dome? You never leave the dome!"

"I know. But I have to take this job."

He frowned, leaning against the back of his sofa and crossing his arms, his biceps bunching with the move. "Why do you have to take it? Is someone going to go with you? You've never even been out there!"

Now I was starting to get irritated. "No, I've never been out there," I agreed. "But I can read a map. And I know how to take care of myself."

He uncrossed his arms and held up his hands in a placating gesture. "I know you can handle yourself. If the job was in the city dome, I wouldn't worry." I knew that wasn't true, but I let him continue. "But out there, you are not at the top of the food chain. Even apart from the dragons and the phoenixes." He shook his head. "Can you delay it for a few days? I can come with you and—"

"I can't delay it," interrupted him. "It's an urgent job."

He narrowed his eyes at me, straightening. "What aren't you telling me?"

I looked away. "Nothing."

Silence.

"At least have the decency to lie well," he murmured.

"Fine. Don't tell me. Do you at least know where you're headed?"

I nodded. Santiago had sent me more information after I'd accepted the job. I brought up my watch and slid through my inbox to find the map. "Here," I said tapping where I needed to go.

Jacob came over to my side, his eyes focused on the map. "You're going to have to go right through dragon territory," he said neutrally.

I frowned, staring at the map. "No, I was planning on heading in this direction around here," I said tracing my finger along the route that I had planned to take.

Jacob shook his head slowly. "That's very rough terrain. You'll lose too much time and your car might not even make it. And this area here is known to be riddled with thieves and slavers." That didn't sound good. "No, your best bet is to go directly through dragon territory. It would cut your time and the path is much smoother."

"How would I get through without them noticing?" I asked, frowning. Cutting right through their territory sounded suicidal. Everyone knew both of the races out there were very protective of their land.

"They rely a lot on sight," he explained. "If you go through at night and keep the noise level down, you could sneak through. I know it's been done before in other territories, so it could possibly be done here. It's not foolproof," he warned. "But I'd say it's safer than that other trail you wanted to go on, though that isn't saying much." He stared at the map some more biting his lip. "Either path is risky as hell though. I repeat—you shouldn't go at all, let alone by yourself. Please wait for me. I'd leave right now with you, but I have some obligations that I can't get out of." From time to time, Jacob would disappear. He was pretty tight-lipped about was he was doing, but he always let me know he'd be gone. I was guessing it had something to do with his previous life. "You need someone with you who knows what it's like out there."

I shook my head. There was no doubt Jacob would be excellent backup. But considering what was out there, "If I get caught by dragons, how would you be able to help?" I asked reasonably, closing the map. "The advice is really appreciated, but if shit hits the fan out there-- "

His jaw tightened and he stepped back, his face cool. "Fine." He turned away from me and walked over to the window. "You're a closed book, I understand that. I give you your space. I never push you when you shut down." He braced an arm against the wall. "But I wish you would tell me what was actually going on here. You aren't stupid. This isn't like you."

I sighed. He was right. But that didn't mean I could tell him anymore. I didn't have anyone I trusted more in my life, but caution was my byword. I would love to have someone at my back but I needed to leave now, as per the job's guidelines.

But, more importantly, I couldn't risk anyone else finding out what I truly was. Even Jacob. My skin in the direct sunlight would give me away if anyone was too close. There was no mistaking the metallic sheen. I'd have to just leave things like this. And it sucked. It really did. This was why I resisted friendships so hard.

"Bye, Jacob," I finally said quietly.

He didn't respond. I left his place, hoping I hadn't lost the only friend I really had.

Back in my own bed, I didn't sleep well at all. When I finally shut my brain off long enough to rest, it was like I had just managed to close my eyes when my alarm went off once again.

Gritty-eyed and grim, I dressed.

It was time to go the address Santiago had sent me. I

walked over there, intending to bring whatever the mysterious package was back to my apartment and then load up the car. At least it wasn't too far. The place I ended up at looked like an office building. One much nicer than my own.

My watch dinged and I glanced down to click on the message.

The package is inside waiting in the lobby.

All right.

Frowning, I climbed up a flight of clean stairs and stepped in past beveled glass doors. Fancy. The lobby inside had a twenty-foot-tall ceiling and was way bigger than any I'd ever seen.

Completely unnecessary. But space was a clear indication of wealth and they were definitely trying to broadcast that they had it here. Mission accomplished.

There were a couple of people waiting in the overstuffed chairs to the side, but I didn't pay them much attention as I walked straight up to the receptionist sitting behind the counter. The red hair she had swept up into a sleek bun came from a salon rather than a box, and it suited her pale skin. She gave me a polite smile when I reached her.

"May I help you?" she inquired, her eyes tracking down my beat-up jacket and even-more-beat-up boots. Probably observing I didn't match the mostly white color palette in here.

"I'm here to pick up a package," I said.

"Oh, yes. Miss Hill?" she asked.

"Yes."

"Perfect." She leaned to the side and looked into the seating area. "Omari!"

I frowned and turned to see who she was calling.

A small child, maybe six or so, stood up and started walking towards me. He was of mixed race, and his skin was a warm, golden brown. His large eyes were a darker shade of brown. As he drew closer, I took in his sweet face and the beat-up nature of his t-shirt, jeans, and shoes. The backpack he carried had also seen better days. Everything was of good quality, so I was guessing it was just well-loved.

"There's been a mistake," I said slowly. "I'm here for a package. Not a child."

The receptionist frowned, looking at her computer screen. "I was told a Miss Hill would be here to pick up Omari Watson at seven in the morning." She looked back at me with an expression that said this wasn't her problem.

The kid reached me just as my watch dinged again. Gritting my teeth, I opened the new message. It was from Santiago. Surprise, surprise.

Omari Watson is half phoenix and half human. His mother has died, and he is suffering from sun sickness. He needs to leave the city dome to reach his family, who will take him in.

I looked down at Omari's face and noted the pallor under the warmth of the skin. He also looked a little sweaty even though the lobby was cool.

"One second," I said, turning and taking a few strides away.

I spoke into the microphone in my watch to dictate a return message.

I don't deliver live goods.

It didn't take long for me to get a response.

You will deliver Omari. I've procured a vehicle for your trip. It is waiting in the garage under the building.

Shit.

I turned back to Omari. He looked so small and alone as he stood next to the reception desk, his eyes wide as he watched me. If nothing else, I needed to get him into the sun as quickly as I could.

I walked back over to him and sank down into a crouch so I could be at eye level.

"Hi, Omari. My name is Mia. I'm here to take you to your family. Are you ready to go?"

He nodded, staying silent.

All right then.

I stood and he immediately raised his hand up. I took the small, soft hand in mine. This was getting more and more complicated.

I turned back to the receptionist. "How do I get to the garage?"

"Take the elevator at the end of the hall down to the basement. Your vehicle should be waiting for you."

I nodded and hustled Omari over to the elevator. It was small, with mirrored doors and tufted panels on the bottom half of the walls. I'm sure it was meant to appear opulent but it reminded me of a padded cell.

The doors opened, and we walked out into a well-lit garage. Directly in the space in front of us, there was a vehicle that basically boiled down to a tank. About three times as large as my own car, it was meant to be all-terrain judging by the construction. Armored paneling and a desert-camouflage paint job made it stand out like a...well, like a tank among cars.

"Is that our car?" Omari asked in a hushed voice.

I looked down at him, closing my own mouth. "I think so." At least Santiago wasn't stingy.

I walked over to the car and stopped at the retinal scanner mounted at the driver's side door. It asked me for my fingerprint too. Santiago must have keyed me in using records he would have had to obtain illegally. No surprise there.

The locks clicked open.

"Get in," I told Omari as I slid into the driver's side.

He scrambled into the seat next to me, and it immediately moved back.

"Child detected," the car informed me in a smooth female voice.

Perfect.

"Put on your seat belt, Omari," I murmured as I did the same. "We're going to head back to my place and then to the market."

He nodded, watching me.

Should I say something else? I had no real experience with children.

"Are you okay?" I tried.

"Yes." He kept staring at me.

All right then.

I started the car under his watchful gaze and pulled out of the spot. It moved surprisingly smoothly for something so large and undoubtedly heavy.

And away we went.

God help us.

CHAPTER FOUR

I drove the car up the street, trying not to hit any of the pedestrian traffic. This was why I didn't like driving my car.

Maryam's face when I stopped the tank in front of her stall was almost worth it.

"What are we doing here?" Omari asked, his eyes glued to the window as he looked around.

"Getting supplies," I said.

"Can I come?" he asked in a small voice, fastening hopeful eyes on me.

Sighing, I nodded. I was probably setting a bad precedent.

"Come out this way." I didn't want him exiting the car on the traffic side. He scrambled over to the driver's side, and I helped him down to the ground.

"Nice car," Maryam commented as we walked up to her stall, Omari's hand in mine.

"Thanks. It's on loan for the job."

"Maybe you can have them throw it in at the end," she suggested with a wink as she gestured to a couple of her assistants to carry the water out to the car. "And who is this little guy?" she asked, her eyes falling on Omari.

"I'm Omari," he said in a confident voice, looking around at all the interesting things she had on view. "What's that?" he asked, pointing at something.

I followed the line of his small finger to a stylized knife scabbard. One with naked figures going at it, arms and limbs entwined. Yeesh.

"That's just a knife," I said quickly, moving him over to my other side, out of view of it. "Don't worry about it." I turned back to Maryam who looked like she was suppressing a smile. Glad someone was enjoying this. "I'm going to need more rations. Suitable for a child."

Maryam's eyebrows went up at that. "You're taking him out of the dome?" she asked.

"Yes. Reasons."

She looked doubtful, but she moved to the back and came out with some other boxes.

"The stuff I gave you is fine for kids, but here's some that might taste better to him. Here, let me throw you some snacks too. They might not last too long in this heat, but that thing you just pulled up in should keep them fine for a while."

I took everything she gave me and then we were good to go.

"Come on, Omari," I said, taking his hand. "Time to get going."

He didn't argue with me. He just clambered back into his seat and put his seat belt on. Fast learner.

I put the car back into gear and slowly crept through traffic to get to one of the two exterior gates. I'd gone through it a lot, at least twice a week for the entirety of my life. But it was different this time. I knew I wasn't just going out for an hour or so in a nearby area. I knew I'd be spending at least two weeks out there.

And now I had more than just myself to worry about.

Omari had his face plastered against the window again, watching the other cars. I shook my head, smiling despite myself as I faced forward. He didn't act like a kid who'd just lost his mother. Then again, I hadn't cried much either when I'd gone through the same thing. Everyone dealt differently. Though he seemed fine, I would definitely suggest a counselor to his family when I saw them.

If I saw them.

I needed to be optimistic.

The line to the gate inched forward as cars moved through the two rooms on the way out. The atmosphere of the first chamber was controlled and the second one was not, though the airflow was adjusted so that it didn't mix with the air from the first room. Everything was set up to make sure the controlled environment of the dome remained controlled.

The caustic chemicals in the air outside the dome weren't just bad for general health, but also for wear and tear of everyday things like plastics and metals. The pollution humanity created was what caused the ozone to deplete to such a state that they needed to build these city domes to survive. A full human couldn't stand out in those rays without some kind of physical protection for more than five minutes at a time if he or she didn't want to risk radiation burns.

Even now, everyone wore head-to-toe sun-protective clothing if they needed to leave the dome. I had a set, for appearances, though I never wore it.

Phoenixes and dragons remained outside the domes. Their hardier natures let them breathe the air without fear, and their need for the sun kept them outside. No one knows where they came from, they were just a part of life nowadays, but people say they didn't exist before the radiation.

I brought the car to a stop in front of the security station right before the gate.

"Retinal scan," the guard intoned, his tone and demeanor bored.

I obligingly put my window down and set my face in front of the scanner. It flashed my identity across the screen.

The guard checked it and nodded. "Proceed."

"Thank you."

I'd done the same a million times before, but every time I went through security, adrenaline flooded my body with heat.

We reached the first chamber, and the large metal-and-glass gate slowly slid to the side to let us through. The gate closed behind us with growling whoosh due to the seal.

Omari made a small sound. He was hunched in his chair.

"Don't worry. That's just the air," I said, trying to reassure him.

He didn't look very reassured. But we'd be through in a moment.

The rushing sound of wind hit us as powerful fans created a wall of moving air across the gate leading to the next room. The cross flow would prevent the air between the two chambers from mixing. The next gate opened, revealing the other room, with the same cement floors and glass and metal walls. I drove into it and stopped once again as the gate behind us closed.

Then the final gate opened, the almost-blinding sun shining into the comparative dimness of the room we were in.

"Here we go," I muttered to myself.

I drove out, my eyes adjusting to the brightness.

Flat, bleached desert stretched out in every direction, with hazy mountains rising in the distance. The sky above was white-blue, the sun's heat brutal as it beat down upon the dusty and cracked earth. There wasn't any life to be seen apart from some hardy cacti and smaller bugs that could apparently survive anything.

The road that led away from the dome was straight ahead of us, but I took a fainter path moving away at an angle.

Omari needed sun now. I wanted to make sure he was in full health before we continued, and this vehicle was made to keep light out. So I took the car to the spot behind a large rock that I used when I needed to be outside. Santiago had proved to me that this place wasn't as safe as I'd thought, but he was the only one who knew about it. I hoped.

"Why are we stopping?" Omari asked, confused. He was already looking worse than when I first picked him up, the grayish cast to his skin more pronounced.

"We're stopping so you and I can both get some sun," I said, even though I was good for another couple of days.

"Oh, okay!" he said, reaching for the door.

I stepped outside and helped him down.

"Take off your shirt and your pants," I ordered as I peeled my own shirt off.

He didn't argue, taking off his clothes efficiently enough, leaving him in his cartoon-character underwear. Maximum skin exposure would mean we would need less time under the actual rays of the sun.

His warm brown skin glinted copper in sunlight, a clear indication of his phoenix heritage. My own skin shimmered in the light too. It was neither copper like a phoenix nor gold like a dragons. I attributed that to a quirk of being mixed.

This was exactly the reason why I couldn't have anyone else out here with me. The shine coming off both Omari's skin and my own was a dead giveaway. No one who saw us now would believe we were human. Or at least not fully so.

"Why don't you move onto that rock and lie down?" I suggested.

The rock would be hot from the sun, but as even half phoenix, Omari would have a high tolerance for heat.

"Okay!" he chirped.

I lifted him up and helped him get settled on the rock, on his back so that he would have the most surface area.

I climbed up and sat down next to him, opening up the map. If Jacob hadn't warned me of the other route, I would've taken it. I still might have taken it if not for my "package". The danger that awaited me out here was less about humans and more about dragons. But now I had a child to consider.

Going directly through the dragons' territory meant that I would shorten the trip by a significant amount of time. It wasn't good for Omari to be out here like this, vulnerable, any longer than necessary. And Jacob was right. If I was careful, and drove through at night, I should be able to drive through most of the dragon territory before the sun rose once again.

Theoretically.

It wasn't a perfect plan. But I couldn't come up with a better one. And this car that wanted to be a tank was actually surprisingly quiet.

I sighed as I looked up.

I was going to have to just cross my fingers and hope for the best. We would stay on that sun-drenched rock for an hour. We couldn't spare more time than that. Then I would set out in the most direct route to the nearest phoenix territory. If my timing was right, we would hit the dragon boundary just after nightfall, giving us the whole night to get through.

I closed the map and looked over at Omari where he was lying next to me. His eyes were closed and there was a slight smile on his face as he soaked in the sun. His skin was already losing that grayish tinge, health seeping back into his face.

Relief washed through me at the clear indication he was doing better. I lay down next to him in my sports bra and boy shorts. I might as well enjoy the time in the sun, too.

Finding a moment to relax was going to become difficult soon.

CHAPTER FIVE

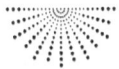

*B*y the time we hit dragon territory, the sun had been gone for about half an hour.

I turned off my lights twenty minutes before I expected the boundary, not wanting to risk being a beacon for anything flying by. Luckily, the moon and starlight was just bright enough for me to see any obstacles while crawling forward at a slow, excruciating pace. Amari was already asleep next to me, which was for the best. There wasn't really much to see now that the sun had set. Not that there was much when the sun was out either.

Just as I was wondering if maybe I'd been wrong about crossing the boundary and had taken a wrong turn somewhere, the outline of a building showed dimly on the horizon. As if I just needed to see that one to see the others, all at once the skyline of a sprawling city appeared.

The dragon stronghold was situated in the middle of an old city, part of it in ruins and part of it in use by the dragons. There was no way to completely avoid the whole thing unless I still wanted to be in their territory come daytime, so my goal was to go through the unoccupied parts in the hopes that I would make it out unseen.

Piece of cake.

Had I really thought this was a viable plan? It had seemed so much more possible in the safety of the dome.

I took in the jagged outlines of buildings that had fallen into disrepair. The part that was still in use must have been farther in. At the pace that we were progressing forward, it would take me another thirty minutes to hit the edge of the city proper. It was agonizing to go so slowly while we were in the open, but I didn't want to hit anything accidentally and draw attention.

The night was still quiet around me. I had lowered the windows and opened the hatch above us so we could hear if anything happened. A still night was all that greeted me so far.

A whimper had me looking over at Omari. He was frowning, curled up into a ball in the seat. He must have been having a nightmare.

To comfort him, I set a gentle hand on his shoulder.

Mistake.

His eyes snapped open and he bolted upright in his seat. He sucked in a large breath and let it out in a piercing scream so loud that the echoes of it bounced back from the city in front of us.

Shit.

I stopped the car and hit the buttons to close the windows and the hatch above us, though I already knew it was too late.

"Omari!" I said urgently, taking hold of his small shoulders. His eyes were still a little glazed over as he kept screaming. "Omari, look at me!" I repeated more loudly, shaking him gently to get his attention. His screams finally died down as his eyes focused and he saw my face. I unbuckled his seat belt and brought him over onto my lap to hug him. His arms wrapped around me.

"It's okay," I murmured, as I looked out the windshield and the side windows. "It's okay."

I doubted it was okay. Those screams were loud enough to broadcast our location for miles. With any luck, the darkness and the desert-camouflage paint on the car would hide us enough so that we wouldn't be seen. I reached up to open the hatch on the top of the car a little so I could hear better.

Omari sat quietly in my lap with his head tucked up against my shoulder, his heartbeat still fast.

A moment passed. Another.

Nothing.

Maybe we got lucky...

But then there was a sound, a slight shift in the air, a barely-there change in the air pressure.

Swallowing dryly, I looked up at the shadowy shape and my heart almost stopped.

The moonlight etched its outline in silver, highlighting the yards-long wingspan and the sinuous body. Its head was as sleek as the rest of it, built to slice through the air, its tail narrow and mobile.

I watched as it turned to circle above us. Maybe it didn't see us.

A deep rumble broke through the air.

All right.

There was some chance that we'd been spotted.

CHAPTER SIX

"**O**mari, you need to get back into your seat and put your seat belt on, okay?" I murmured, my eyes still in the sky.

"Are there dragons outside?" he asked in a hushed whisper.

No use lying. He could just look through the window or the hatch.

"Yes," I said, helping him into his seat and pulling the seat belt over to secure him into place. "I'm going to go fast now," I said, and checked my own seat belt again.

He nodded, his eyes glued to the open hatch above us.

Here we go.

Putting the car back into gear, I slammed the pedal down. It lurched into motion. Chances of escaping were slim to none, but I had to try. Maybe if I could make it to the unused part of the city, I could take cover somewhere with Omari.

I had to protect him from them. Dragons and phoenixes were enemies. It was one of the facts everyone knew. Like the sky was blue. Or the air outside the domes wasn't good for humans.

Another roar and staccato growl came from above us. I was unable to resist looking up. Three more shapes were now gliding soundlessly through the air.

Clenching my jaw, I turned my attention back to the space ahead.

We hit a large rock and bounced over it, my teeth snapping shut from the abruptness. There was a reason why I hadn't been going faster than a crawl before. But now I was willing to risk it.

Omari gasped and I reached over so he could hold my hand. His small ones immediately took a tight hold on me.

Just a little further...

The sound of beating wings filled the night air.

I chanced another glance up and found more dragon-shapes lazily following the car. At any moment, one of them could choose to simply burn us. The armor was fire resistant, but not fireproof. No armor was. It could take a glancing blow but it couldn't take direct, sustained fire.

If it was just me in the car, I would have made peace that this was the end. I was an adult and my choices led me to this moment, where there were no choices left.

But I wasn't the only one the car. Giving up wasn't an option.

"Come on," I muttered to myself, trying to will the car to go faster. I frowned. Was the city moving?

No...the world was tilting...

Was the car flipping? Had I hit a rock?

A gust of hot wind blew my hair across my eyes. Oh no. My hand tightened on the wheel as I looked up.

Right into the underside of a dragon.

I squeezed Omari's hand as I looked out the windshield and realized we were being lifted. One of the dragons had literally taken hold of the car and was picking us up. I couldn't even fathom how much strength that took.

Heart in my throat, I watched the world fall away, until the roofs of the buildings in the city were below us. It was larger than I'd thought it was. From this vantage point, it was clear that the inhabited part of the city was directly in the center of the vast ruins.

It was built taller, with the new parts showing above the older buildings, but I'd been too far away to make them out at night. It was also somewhat shielded from view by the unoccupied portions. The lower part of the center section was lit and people were walking around even at this time of night. They must have installed windows to deliberately block light in the upper floors of the tall buildings, to minimize how visible they were at night. It made sense as a security measure.

In one corner of that area, there was a flat, round clearing with tall walls encircling it. That was where our impromptu pilot took us.

The dragon slowly came to a hovering standstill above the clearing and carefully lowered us down onto the ground. The care with which the tires connected suggested that they weren't trying to kill us.

At least not immediately.

Maybe they were just waiting to interrogate me before incinerating us.

What a reassuring thought.

The round clearing was much larger than I'd realized from up above. The six dragons that were following us had plenty of room. The dragon that had picked us up landed directly in front of us. It lowered its long neck almost down to the ground and tilted its head to regard me through the windshield.

Its head was almost as big as the car.

I looked over to see that Omari had his eyes squeezed

shut. I had the urge to do the same. I'd never seen a dragon or phoenix in their other form. Not in person.

The idea of a dragon had always seemed otherworldly, majestic. But the reality of the sheer size of it, of the power behind that enormous body, the intelligence behind those eyes...

Next to this giant, I seemed small and insignificant. Any one of those things could kill me in an instant without breaking a sweat. The idea of going after one with my bow and arrow was preposterous now that I was so close. How was I supposed to take one down with something so small?

It was dim, but I could see each individual scale, the three-foot-long talons at the end of each toe, the sharpness of the fangs when it opened its mouth slightly.

I took a deep breath. I needed to keep calm. Freaking out wouldn't accomplish anything, even if that was really all I wanted to do.

I took another deep breath and let it out. I needed to see what they wanted.

Hopefully it wasn't a fresh, barbecued meal.

CHAPTER SEVEN

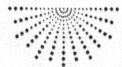

*T*he dragon in front of us straightened and lifted its head.

It was a little brighter here, so I could just make out that he or she was probably a golden color. The others arranged around us in a circle also seemed to be various shades of gold, though none of them seemed to be quite as brilliant a gold as the first. At least as far as I could tell in this lighting. For all I knew they weren't gold at all but silver.

Not that any of that really mattered at this moment.

It wasn't like I was going to file a police report when I got back describing exactly what kind of dragon it was that picked up my car after I'd invaded dragon territory.

My attention returned to the dragon directly in front of us. Something about its positioning and the fact that it was slightly bigger than the rest told me that it was the one in charge.

I didn't have to wonder long.

A second later, the air around the dragon seemed to almost ripple, like heat emanating from the ground. I blinked as I watched, not knowing quite what I was seeing.

It was like my eyes couldn't understand so they didn't see it.

Somehow, between one moment and the next, the massive dragon shape shrunk down into a much smaller one.

A humanoid one. Though small was a relative term.

Yes, the man was much smaller than his dragon form. But he looked to be well above six feet tall, closer to six and a half maybe. Not small by any standards.

And very naked.

As he strode forward towards the car, I took in his still-impressive shape. Broad shoulders narrowed into a slim waist and hips. He was carved down to pure muscle. His arms, the muscled planes of his chest, the cobblestone abs. Even his legs were thick with muscle, though not in the bodybuilding way. No, this was a man whose body was carved through actual effort. Not through steroids or hours with weights.

As he drew closer, I could make out details better. His hair was a little long, dark with light streaks that I couldn't quite make out the color of. His face was...masculine. That was the first word that came to mind. Defined jaw, straight nose, high cheekbones with hollows underneath, slashes of dark brows highlighted light-colored eyes, though I wasn't sure if they were blue or green.

There was no denying that he was a head-turner. In the city dome, women and more than a few men would probably follow him with their eyes when he walked by. As it was, I tried my best not to focus on another very naked part of him.

I guess clothes didn't stay on when they shifted. Which, intellectually, made sense. I just never expected to be faced with that fact so blatantly.

He stopped about ten feet in front of the car, his gaze locked with mine as I sat inside with Omari clutching at my arm.

I stared back, not knowing how to react. I figured silence was a safe bet.

After a moment of staring at each other, he finally opened his mouth. "Get out of the car," he said in a calm, deep voice, the bass rumble of his dragon form hinted at in the tone.

I hesitated, not knowing if I should bring Omari out with me.

"Now," he added, his jaw tight.

Okay.

"Omari," I said quietly, turning to him. "I'm going to have to get out of the car for a second. Can you stay in your seat for now?"

He lifted his head a little, his eyes glancing outside. Swallowing hard, he asked, "Can I stay with you?"

"I'll be right outside," I reassured him. "It's safer for you to stay in here while I talk to them." I cupped the side of his face and leaned down so I could see his eyes. "Okay?"

His eyes were wide as he nodded. He still looked frightened and I didn't blame him. I was frightened myself.

I opened the door and stepped outside, closing it behind myself. Practically, I didn't know if he would be much safer in the car. But it made me worry less having some kind of barrier around him.

I circled around to the front of the car and leaned back against the hood, putting myself between the guy in front of me and the car. I crossed my arms over my chest in an effort to look less terrified but I wasn't fooling anyone.

His eyes scanned down my body, cataloging everything. The glance was swift and efficient, but I knew without a doubt that he would be able to rattle off every detail of my appearance if he had to.

"Who are you?" he asked, making no move to draw closer.

"Mia Hill." Lying would probably not be smart if he had any way to confirm my identity. I didn't know if freely offering more information would be helpful or not, so I decided to simply stick to answering what he asked.

"Mia Hill," he repeated slowly. "What are you doing in my territory, Mia Hill?" His eyes glanced passed my shoulder over to Omari in the vehicle. I stepped to the side to block his view. He raised an eyebrow at me. "With a child no less."

I had to tell them something. After running through various possibilities, I decided the truth would actually serve me the best. I hoped it would be enough.

"I run a carrier business. The job I'm working right now requires that I bring this child to his family. I took a calculated risk and thought it might be faster and safer to bring him through your territory rather than go through the longer route that would take me around you."

He let me say my piece, his eyes focused on my face. The intensity of his attention was a little unnerving. Silence stretched as he considered what I'd said. He shook his head.

"You thought it would be safer to drive through the heart of my territory with the child."

Disbelief was clear in his voice. Considering what had just happened, I couldn't blame him.

I shrugged. "Yes."

He stared at me. "Well, Mia Hill, your calculated risk was stupid," he said bluntly.

My back stiffened. Way to rub it in. Yes, maybe this wasn't ideal but that didn't mean I wanted to have my face rubbed in it. However, for once I kept my mouth shut. Escalating the situation would not be in our best interest.

When I didn't respond, the man took a step closer.

My hand automatically went to the hilt of my dagger at my side.

He raised his eyebrows at that and paused. "If I was going to kill you, you would already be dead," he pointed out bluntly. "If you try to attack me with that tiny knife, you would be dead even if you were to succeed, which you wouldn't. My skein here would take care of you right away." His eyes went back to the car behind me. "And I would rather not have that happen in front of this audience."

My eyes locked with his when they turned back to me, taking his measure. He kept his expression calm and still. I couldn't read him. But everything he'd said was true enough. I let my hand slide away from my knife. It wouldn't help me right now anyway.

He nodded slightly in acknowledgment of the move and closed the distance between us. He stopped maybe a foot and a half away from me. Close enough that I knew exactly how large and intimidating he was. He took in a deep, deliberate breath.

What was he doing?

His eyes narrowed and he took a partial step closer to me still. Right into my personal space. Leaning in he took another breath. Was he smelling me?

Not knowing what else to do, I just stood there, fighting the urge to take a step back. Hey, if all he wanted to do was smell me, I would take that over being engulfed in flames any day.

He finally moved back again, his eyes considering me.

A moment passed.

This guy was really into his dramatic silences.

I forced myself to stay still and not block him as he stepped past me and opened the door to the car. I really wanted to pull him back. He ducked his head inside, but he made no move to actually enter. After a few seconds, he straightened again.

He moved so he was standing in front of me. "My name is Ashur Jah. I am the Dragon Lord for this area. You and the child will be my guests tonight."

There was a formality in that statement that made it

sound official somehow. And there was no hint of invitation in his tone. It was clearly an order.

"That's very gracious of you," I tried, carefully. "But I'm trying to make good time."

"You will stay here tonight," he repeated.

My mouth tightened as my eyes locked with his. I really didn't like being told what to do. I also wasn't stupid, despite what he might believe. Sometimes there was no choice.

"We'd love to," I said, unable to completely keep the sarcasm from my voice.

The corners of his mouth twitched. "I'm glad to hear it," he replied seriously.

He turned and gestured to someone lurking in the shadows. Or multiple someones. A man and a woman, both dressed in t-shirts and jeans, walked over. At least they weren't naked.

"Hathai and Enzi will show you to your room."

A petite woman and a wiry, dark-haired man both nodded at me. If someone had told me the day before that I was going to be experiencing dragon hospitality, I would have laughed. As it was, I couldn't find much humor in the situation.

I turned to the car, opened the door, and leaned in.

"Come on, Omari," I called out to him. "We're staying here tonight." I hoped it would be only tonight.

He scrambled across to the driver's side and latched on to me. I grunted. That was a strong grip. I stood up holding him, though I could probably let go since he was now attached with both arms and legs. He looked around for a moment, but then buried his face against my neck.

"Are they going to eat us?" he whispered.

But, apparently, it wasn't quietly enough. The Dragon Lord still heard.

"We don't eat children," Ashur said gently, amusement clear in his voice.

Omari looked over my shoulder at him. "Promise?"

Ashur nodded. "I promise."

Omari's hold on me loosened a little. "Okay." That apparently settled things to his satisfaction.

I turned to follow our guides out of what amounted to a stage or a playing field.

Now that I wasn't so focused on Ashur, I realized we were in some kind of theater. The curved sides along the edges of the packed-earth circle hosted benches at an incline so the view would be clear to anyone sitting down, even in the back.

What did they use this place for? I puzzled over that as we neared the edge of the circle, where our guides had emerged. My neck tingled as we reached the darker shadows. I glanced back over my shoulder.

Ashur was watching us as we walked away, his gaze intense and steady.

I turned away, shivering a little. That wasn't a man I wanted to cross. No matter how gentle he seemed towards Omari, he was a predator.

And he didn't even pretend to hide it.

CHAPTER EIGHT

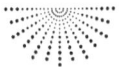

*H*athai and Enzi led us out of the arena through part of the city that looked completely different. Each structure was so tall that I was surprised I hadn't spotted them before.

The streets were much wider than I was used to, though I supposed out here they had all the room they wanted to work with. They weren't constrained with any kind of physical boundary.

Streetlights were placed at even intervals, their soft glow lighting the way.

Something was different. It took me a moment to realize what it was. There was no delineation between the road and the sidewalk. That made me frown.

"No sidewalks?" I asked.

Enzi answered, "We rarely use cars. Wings are much more efficient."

Well, that put me in my place. Maybe driving a car right through the streets here hadn't been the best idea then. Though maybe if I'd hugged the seemingly empty ruins on the edges. Now I would never know.

There were a few people walking along the well-lit road, their eyes following us curiously. More than a couple of them lifted their noses and sniffed discreetly. I was starting to wonder if I needed a shower or something. I bent my head to my shoulder and sniffed at my shirt. Smelled okay to me. I moved Omari from one hip to the other. Carrying a sturdy six-year-old was a bit more taxing than toting a slim briefcase.

As I continued walking, passing by pretty stoops that led to well-maintained and brightly colored doors, something else struck me. Everything was so clean. There wasn't even a little bit of litter anywhere. Even the better areas inside the dome had some dirt, candy wrappers, something. With that much humanity crammed so close together, it was almost impossible to keep everything perfect.

I didn't see anything like that here. It was impressive.

Whatever they use for paving wasn't dark. It was a beige, sand-like color.

"No asphalt?" I asked.

It was Enzi who answered me again. Maybe Hathai wasn't my biggest fan. Or maybe she was just a woman of few words.

"We use a blend that includes desert sand," Enzi explained. "The dark asphalt absorbs too much heat out here."

That made sense. The buildings around us were also built from a light material, not quite the same tone as the ground. I wouldn't be able to tell the exact color until the morning though.

We finally stopped in front of a large building with double doors that were already open, light spilling out onto the stairs leading up.

"Right this way."

I climbed up the stairs, shifting Omari in my arms again. The state of the streets should have clued me in, but I still wasn't expecting how the building looked on the inside. Marble lined the floors, matching the columns. I followed one of them up to the cathedral ceiling, where a pretty mural of the sky covered the space. A large chandelier with sparkling crystals threw soft light all across the room. Furniture was set up in conversational groupings on top of plush area rugs. Paintings adorned the walls, spaced apart and lit individually to set off the rich colors.

Straight ahead, a wide staircase was carpeted in deep purple with a subtle golden pattern woven through it. The stairs rose up and then split halfway, separating into two flights leading to the second story. There was another, slightly smaller chandelier at the landing where the staircase divided. The banisters gleamed under the light, a faux wood that looked different than any I'd seen before.

"Is this a hotel?" I asked. I didn't know who would be staying in the dragon stronghold. Maybe visiting dragons?

Omari wiggled in my arms and I let him down and took his hand. He looked around with the same kind of absorption that I had. I'd never seen a place this nice before.

"No. This is Ashur's home," Enzi explained. "Your room is going to be on the second floor."

All of this belonged just to Ashur? Guess it paid to be at the top of the dragon heap. I didn't know why I was so surprised. Intellectually, I knew the dragons wouldn't live in the actual ruins of the city. But I guess I thought where they did live would be sort of like ruins, if that made sense. I definitely didn't picture this well-thought-out, elegant setup that was a large step above city dome life.

Obviously, my bias was showing. There was no denying that both dragons and phoenixes were painted as somewhat animalistic and less sophisticated or intelligent than humans in most city dome schools.

I didn't realize I'd actually bought into that narrative, knowing my own not-so-human blood. But I guess it still had an effect on me. It made me wonder how many of my other assumptions or ideas might be wrong.

Omari and I followed our guides up the stairs and into a hallway, gently lit and carpeted with the same plush purple. The wallpaper had little gold accents and there were alcoves at regular intervals that housed small benches and paintings. I didn't know who would stop in the hall to take a rest on those benches, but I couldn't deny that the effect was pretty.

"Here we are," Enzi said, stopping in front of a double door. He opened one side. "Unless you would like two rooms?" he asked, looking over at me.

I shook my head. I would keep Omari nearby.

"Wow!" Omari exclaimed as he walked into the room. There was no word for it other than opulent.

The space was large enough that I could have easily fit five of my apartments in it, if not more. The carpet in here was a beautiful cream color, and my boots sank into the plush depths of it as I followed Omari inside. There was a massive four-poster bed with deep gray linens and white trim in the center of the room, with a mountain of accent pillows set up in front of the crisp, white pillowcases. There was a desk in the corner with a delicate chair in front of it and a sleek computer on top.

My watch wouldn't work this far out from the city dome. They must have their own network. Of course they would. It only made sense. I needed to stop being surprised.

A seating area on the other side of the room was complete with a couch and overstuffed chairs and a coffee table in the middle. A tapestry was all the art in this room, the large surface area of it covering almost the entirety of one wall. It depicted dragons sweeping down over the city, only the ruins visible.

Maybe it was a way to remind me where I was. Not that I could forget.

There were two other doors apart from the door leading to the hall. I walked over to one and peeked inside. It was a walk-in closet with a few clothes hanging inside. I could probably live in the closet alone.

Enzi said, "Feel free to help yourself to the clothing there. They aren't anything fancy, but you should be able to find something that fits. I'll bring something more for Omari here." He glanced over at Omari and smiled.

Either everyone was doing their best impersonation of empathetic people, or they really didn't kill phoenix children here.

Call me paranoid, but I wouldn't let my guard down just yet.

I moved over to the other door and turned on the light inside. It was a massive bathroom complete with a tub large enough for five and a separate shower. There were double sinks and more marble, with gold accents in the faucets and the towel rods.

Both the tub and the shower were calling my name but I stepped back outside and turned to face Enzi. His fellow babysitter must have been waiting outside.

"Thank you." Might as well be polite to our captors. I looked over at Omari. "Are you hungry?"

He nodded, looking back over his shoulder at me from where he was poking at the bedspread. I looked at Enzi.

"I'll bring something up for you." He hesitated for a moment before continuing. "And please. Do not leave this room tonight."

I didn't respond, but he took my silence for agreement I suppose, leaving and closing the door behind himself.

"Mia?"

"Hmmm?"

"Are they going to let us go?" he asked, his eyes worried.

"Yes," I said confidently, though I wasn't sure at all. There was no reason for both of us to be worried. He gave me a long look but he let it go. Nothing could have made me feel smaller than having a six-year-old allow me to keep up appearances.

He walked over to the curtains and pushed them open. I thought they covered a window, but with them pushed aside, it was clear there was a balcony outside. Omari immediately opened the door. I quickly followed him outside, not knowing if it was safe for him out there. I tested the railing by shaking it hard, and it didn't budge. Good enough.

Since the buildings where built so high and we were only on the second floor, we couldn't look out over the city. We did have a good view of the street below. Something shiny caught my eye to one side of the balcony—there was a slim ladder bolted to the side of the building that led to the very top.

Easy roof access.

When I looked up, I also realized there were no plain windows, at least not on this side. They were all balconies. I guess when you could fly, not having a balcony would be restricting.

I looked down at the street again and noticed again exactly how wide they were. The facts clicked together in my head. They were built to accommodate a dragon's wingspan.

Somehow, it was that detail the fully brought home that I wasn't in a familiar place anymore. That I had no idea what the rules were here. No matter what my blood said I was, I was still raised mostly human apart from the excursions to soak in the sun.

There was no point dwelling on it. I'd have to roll with the punches and hope for the best.

I looked over at Omari. "I think you need to take a bath."

His face immediately set into a mutinous expression. "No I don't." He peeked up at me and quickly looked away.

I hid a smile. Leaning down, I pretended to sniff at him. "You're starting to smell," I teased with a smile.

He giggled, his smile bright. "No I'm not!"

I straightened, shrugging. "Well, if you want to be smelly, I can't stop you."

He bit his lip and glanced down at himself. "Well...maybe I could take a really fast bath. Not because I need to," he quickly added. "But because it would be polite."

I nodded solemnly. "I understand," I said gravely. I led the way into the bathroom and started the water for him as he chattered about everything we'd seen so far.

"Do you think Ashur showers?" he asked.

"I'm sure he does," I said mildly.

He looked at the tub of the water and sighed. "Okay," he said glumly.

"Do you need help?" I asked, stepping back.

He shook his head. "I know how to bathe all by myself now," he said proudly.

"That's very impressive."

"I know," he said confidently as he took off his shirt. "I'm an impressive person."

I was still chuckling as I left the bathroom.

There was a knock at the door as I entered the bedroom. Enzi was there with a trolley full of food.

"The chef didn't know what Omari would like, so he gave you all the usual suspects."

I looked at the array of chicken nuggets, french fries, and

what looked like small burgers. Meat was usually grown in labs these days because it was more efficient, but they'd gotten pretty good at it.

Everything looked fresh and smelled delicious. My stomach growled in response. Enzi smiled at the sound but didn't comment on it.

"I'm sure this will be fine. Thank you," I said.

Enzi brought forth a bundle from beneath is arm and handed it to me. "I also brought some clothes that might fit the little guy if he needs them."

I took the stack in my hands. Omari's bag was in the car, along with mine. I hadn't thought to grab it. Probably a side effect of being surrounded by dragons.

"Thank you."

He left the room, closing the door again behind himself. I didn't have any illusions he wouldn't barge in if he needed to, but I appreciated the veneer of politeness.

I took the clothes to the bathroom and set them down on the counter.

"Omari, here's some clothes on the counter for you," I told him. I found the towels underneath and picked one out. "I put a towel here too."

"Okay!"

Not knowing what else to do, I left the bathroom. I didn't really know anything about kids. Would he be able to handle everything himself? I shouldn't have worried. Less than five minutes later, Omari came out dressed in the sweatpants and bright yellow shirt that had been left for him. His eyes went directly to the food.

"Come on, sit next to me," I invited.

He sat down in the chair I pointed to and I made him a plate.

"Is there anything you don't want?"

He shook his head so I set the plate in front of him and he dug in with a voracious appetite.

I completely understood. The travel rations were nutritious, but nobody could call them tasty with a straight face.

I bit into one of the burgers and had to close my eyes. God, it was so good. If nothing else, at least we got to eat well while we were here.

Neither Omari nor I were slow eaters, so we worked through all of the food quickly. I was pretty stuffed, and I could see Omari's eyes already closing. Probably I should have made him brush his teeth. But I figured skipping one time wouldn't hurt. And he was exhausted.

Even apart from everything that had happened, I knew he wasn't completely over his sun sickness yet. I could see the gray creeping in again.

"Time for bed," I said, trying not to show my worry.

He didn't argue, climbing in when I pulled back the covers. I really needed a bath too. But when I moved to leave, he stopped me.

"Can you lie down next to me?" he asked sleepily.

I lay down on top of the covers on the other side so I wouldn't get the sheets dirty underneath.

He put his head on the pillow and was asleep in under two minutes.

I carefully got up and shut off the light in the room, but left the bathroom light on and the door open a crack so a small shaft of light came out into the room. I knew when I was a kid, waking up to a fully dark room was not comforting at all.

"What if they don't want us to leave tomorrow?" Omari whispered, his voice sleepy. Not quite conked out after all.

I lay back down on the bed. "We'll just leave anyway," I said.

"Can we do that?"

Good question. "I'll find a way."

He nodded, snuggling into the pillow. Between one breath and the next, he fell asleep.

I waited a little a bit longer to be sure he wouldn't wake up again. When he didn't, I slid out of bed. I needed to speak to Ashur without Omari listening. I needed to know what he had planned, what was going to happen to us. He hadn't said anything about letting us go tomorrow.

If he thought he could just put me away for the night and I'd stay there obediently, he had another thing coming.

I went to the door that opened to the hallway, hoping it was Enzi out there. I knew it wouldn't be empty. They would have left a guard. When I opened it and peeked outside, I let out a sigh of relief.

Enzi stepped away from the wall on the other side of the hall.

"I'm sorry, but you have to stay in the room," he said, sounding apologetic but firm.

I stepped outside and closed the door behind me. "I'm not going back inside until after you've taken me to talk to Ashur."

He shook his head. "I can't do that. My orders were to make sure—"

"I don't care what your orders were. I have a kid asleep in there and I need to know that he's going to be safe. Take me to Ashur or I'll find him myself," I warned, hoping he didn't call my bluff.

He hesitated. Another push might do it.

"Look, what am I going to do? Stab him with a knife? All he would have to do is transform and step on me."

He sighed, shaking his head. "I'm going to regret this." He turned and started down the hall.

Score. I grinned, falling into step beside him. "Life is full of regrets."

He gave me a sideways glance. "This is where you're supposed to reassure me that I won't regret this," he pointed out dryly.

"Sorry," I said. "You won't regret this," I parroted dutifully.

He shook his head. "You're really bad at that."

"You're not the first person to point that out."

CHAPTER NINE

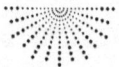

*E*nzi took me down the hall to an elevator this time. When I looked at him questioningly, he explained.

"He's a few floors up. You can take the stairs if you want to, but this is more efficient."

"This is fine."

The gold doors were shiny enough to show us our reflections as we waited.

In silence.

"So...do you get a lot of trespassers?" I asked. I was so amazing at small talk. I watched his reflection look over to me and then turn back to look straight ahead again.

"No."

Good to know. Guess I was in the minority. At least I was special.

We stepped into the elevator and Enzi pressed the button for the forty-fourth floor. My eyebrows rose at that. I guess his definition of a few and mine weren't exactly the same.

We stood in silence again as the elevator rose. Enzi broke it this time.

"You shouldn't push him too much," he said quietly.

"Push who?" I asked, though I had a pretty good idea of who he was talking about.

"Ashur," he confirmed. "He doesn't take kindly to trespassers. You're only alive because you have a child with you."

That was good to know, too. And so comforting.

The doors finally opened into another hall, though this one was short. And the floor wasn't covered in carpet but rather in gleaming faux wood. I looked up from my contemplation of the floor as we walked to the end of the hallway.

What were those sounds?

The hall abruptly opened up into a cavernous space, the ceiling maybe three stories high. Recessed lights illuminated the room, along with sconces around the walls. There were open archways in the middle of every wall in the room, ostensibly leading to other connecting rooms.

On one side of the space, practice mats were laid out on the floor. On the other side, the wall was covered in various weapons. Swords, knives, spears, maces, whips. I didn't know in what scenario a whip would be efficient but there you go.

This was clearly a room set up to train, which was exactly what it was currently being used for. Men and women were focused on exerting themselves, improving their skills. They were dressed in an array of differing outfits. Loose flowing pants, leggings or shorts and sports bras. There didn't seem to be a strict uniform of any kind.

Some were practicing throws and what looked like some form of martial arts on the mats, while others were sparring with weapons or practicing combinations on the heavy bags in the back.

Even among all that activity and all the toned and muscled bodies on display, my eye immediately went to one.

Ashur.

This was the first time I'd seen him in good lighting. His bronze skin gleamed under that illumination, his chest bared but his legs covered in loose, black pants. His focus was on his opponent, a tall but whiplash thin man who had the grace of flowing water.

I watched them attack each other, Ashur's blows fast and powerful, the other man's flowing and almost delicate. The thin man was pretty to look at but Ashur quickly got the upper hand.

His fighting style wasn't elegant or for show. It was brutal and efficient. And it didn't take long before the other man was on the ground with Ashur pinning him. He tapped out and Ashur got back to his feet, lending a helping hand up.

I didn't think he'd noticed our entrance, but as soon as he turned away from his opponent, his eyes zeroed in on me.

I could finally see that they were a pale, crystal-clear blue. At the moment, they were icy cold. His hair was dark with paler gold streaks that looked sun bleached, the length just long enough to fall over his forehead but not long enough to obscure his eyesight. It was cut shorter at the sides and the back.

His eyes took me in and then immediately turned to Enzi. The question was clear.

"She wanted to see you and I would've had to use force to stop her," he explained.

Ashur shook his head as someone threw a towel at him and he used it to wipe down his face and chest on the way over to us.

My eyes fell down to his bare feet. Somehow, even they were sexy. I really needed to get ahold of myself.

He stopped a few feet away from me, tossing the towel into a bin near the door.

"Enzi, you can wait over there."

His eyes didn't move from my face as Enzi shifted away. Now that I was up close, the sheer physicality of him hit me again. He towered over me. And he wasn't just taller. His frame itself was large and he'd packed a good amount of muscle onto it. This was a body honed to fight.

He stared at me for a moment longer and then turned to one of the doorways. "Come with me."

I followed behind him silently, everyone's eyes on me even as they continued to do what they had been doing. I kept my eyes focused on the broad back in front of me, trying not to look down at that butt. I was largely unsuccessful.

The doorway led out to a large balcony that took up the whole side of the building. The night air was cool and fresh, and up this high, it was in motion all around us.

Ashur went up to the ornately carved railing and leaned against it, facing out, even though there were various groupings of places to sit along the length of the balcony. I took my cue and leaned against the railing a few feet down from him. I turned my head to watch his clean profile as he looked out at the city below. I had a sudden image of his dragon form crouched at the top of the building, surveying his domain.

"What did you want to talk to me about?" he asked.

Straight to the point. I could work with that.

"I need to know if you're going to let us go. Not that I don't appreciate your hospitality." That last bit probably wasn't smart to add, but did he expect me to be a happy prisoner?

He nodded, still not looking at me. "Do you know anything about the Phoenix King?" he asked.

I frowned. "What does that have to do with anything?"

He finally turned to face me. "Since that child has phoenix blood, and you're saying you're taking him to meet his family, the only logical conclusion here is that you're going to phoenix territory. So, the question is very relevant."

I tilted my head to the side as I regarded him. My impulse was to tell him that my knowledge or lack thereof was none of his business. But I wasn't exactly on stable ground here. We were in the middle of his territory, in his stronghold, and what happened to us now was completely up to him. It wouldn't be smart to antagonize him, no matter how much my impetuously smart mouth wanted to.

"I don't know much about him," I admitted.

He shook his head. "Then why did you take this job?" he asked, his tone disbelieving and more than a little judgmental.

Okay, that was taking it a little too far. I didn't need his opinion on my choices. He didn't know me. "Now, that really isn't any of your business," I countered, my voice calm. Though I doubted my expression was.

One corner of his mouth tilted up in a smirk. "See, that's where I have to disagree with you. Again. You decided to trespass on my territory. That was a mistake. You are now my business." He closed the distance between us in one long stride, until he was merely inches away. Until the heat from his body washed over my own and the scent of him filled my nose, hot and pure male.

I swallowed, my heartbeat picking up. "I apologize. I won't make the same mistake again."

His smile widened. "I don't think you understand the ramifications of what you did." I froze as his hand reached up and took a lock of my dark hair, sliding it through his fingers. His eyes never left mine. "Trespassers forfeit all rights. I could do anything I wanted and I would be within our laws."

His voice was low, intimate.

I should have been angry. I should have been insulted. But while those emotions were present, they were confused, mixed oddly with others. Doubt. Curiosity.

The whole mess overlaid with an undeniable heat, an attraction I couldn't explain.

The same feeling was mirrored in his eyes. He let me see the heat in them. I didn't know if it was supposed to be a threat, or a way to manipulate me. No matter what the intention, it certainly had an effect. After a few moments of invading my personal space, he took a step back.

I let out a silent breath tinged with relief. And maybe some regret. Because obviously my judgment was completely off in this case.

"I think it's best if you go back to your room now," he said, his eyes going back to the doorway we'd come through. "You should stay there tonight. For your own safety." Then he turned away from me to look back over the city.

I was dismissed. Enzi was already waiting for me. With one last look at Ashur, I walked over to Enzi. I was leaving with only more questions. And no real answers.

Enzi led me back through the practice room. Had they been listening? I met a woman's eyes, and she quickly looked away.

Of course they had.

Enzi led me back to the bank of elevators and we stepped inside. He waited for the doors to close.

"I hope you got the answer you were looking for. Ashur isn't exactly happy with me."

I shook my head. "I don't know if I got the answer I was looking for. But I got something," I murmured.

He glanced over at me. I could sense his hesitation.

"You should be careful," he finally said as elevator doors opened and we walked down the carpeted hall to my room. "You're already playing with fire by just being here."

I opened the door and looked back at him. "Maybe," I acknowledged. "But it seems to me I'm already in the fire." I stepped into the dark room and closed the door behind me.

I didn't know what to focus on as I found a pair of pajamas in the closet and took a shower. I slid into bed next to Omari, the future no clearer than when I'd left. But the events of the last couple of days had caught up with me. I closed my eyes.

And despite everything, I slept.

I'd deal with tomorrow when it came.

CHAPTER TEN

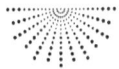

When I woke up the next morning, I had more immediate concerns to worry about. Omari's breathing was shallow and his skin was coated in a light layer of sweat. With my heart in my throat, I leaned over to shake him awake.

He opened his eyes halfway, their gaze unfocused.

"Wake up, Omari. Let's go outside," I urged, trying to keep the fear out of my voice.

He closed his eyes again. "Tired," he muttered.

My worry immediately ramped up to panic, and I slid my arms under his slight weight and picked him up, cradling him to my chest. I leaned against the wall to shove my feet into my boots, and then I shifted him in my arms so I could open the door.

Hathai was in the hall now rather than Enzi. She looked at me, but then her eyes moved down to Omari.

"I need access to the sun. Now," I barked, beyond politeness.

If she gave me any problems right now, I'd be more than happy to punch her in the face and find a way out myself.

"Follow me," she said turning and jogging down the hall.

Okay then. That was a lot easier than I expected. She took me to the elevator and pressed the button for the rooftop.

"We're almost there Omari," I murmured, pulling him in closer.

Hathai was watching me closely. I had no idea what she was thinking. That was one hell of a poker face.

It took some time to get all the way up to the top and every second grated on my nerves. Finally, the doors opened directly to the sun-drenched roof.

"Over here," Hathai directed.

The rooftop was much larger than I thought it would be. The edges extended out past the building's footprint by quite a bit. Taking in the space with a glance, I followed Hathai over to the right side where there was a row of beds already made with crisp white linens. Their spare frames were made of stiff plastic, probably so they didn't absorb too much heat. They were all empty right now, but they must have been here for this very reason.

I set Omari down on the first bed I reached and stripped off his shirt and pants to maximize sun exposure. He sighed as the warmth hit him and turned his head to the side.

"I don't understand. He was fine yesterday," I said, at a loss.

"Sometimes it's unpredictable with children. Some need more sun than others and take longer to fully recover," she explained, her eyes on Omari. "I have no idea about part-human children. That's one more wrench in the works."

She glanced up at me and frowned. The golden metallic sheen of her skin was suddenly visible in the bright daylight. I realized I was in short sleeves, with my face and arms completely exposed in direct sunlight.

Shit. Too late to do anything about that now.

I ignored the look, sitting down on the edge of the bed next to Omari.

"I'll stay here with him if you want to go down and shower or have breakfast," she offered after it was apparent I wasn't going to leave.

I didn't have any reason to believe she would do anything to harm him. Or that anyone here would hurt him. But...

"I'm just going to stay here. But thank you."

She nodded, as if she understood. "I'll have breakfast brought up for you."

"Thank you."

She left me on the roof. I guess she figured that there was no way for me to leave from here without being caught. But then I discovered something. There were guards stationed on every corner of the rooftop. I had been so focused on Omari that I didn't even realize they were there. Dressed in clothes that blended with the bleached-out rooftop, and standing so still, they were easy enough to miss. One of them had turned to watch me, but the others were all facing outward.

Okay then.

I guess looking down the side of the building for that ladder was out of the question. Not that I could leave with Omari in this state anyway. Apart from the beds up here, there were also multiple seating arrangements, complete with sofas and tables. There was even a bar over on one side. It seemed like every section of this building was made to accommodate people.

One entire side of the rooftop had no railing. It was just a ledge—a very high ledge. Just seeing it made me want to step back, even though I was yards and yards away from it. I'm sure it was convenient if you had wings. All I could think about was accidentally falling and going splat in that nice wide street down there.

Better to look away. I turned my attention to the view

instead. From this vantage point, the tops of the other buildings around us were bright in the sun. There was a clear delineation between the part of the city that was used and the part that was left in ruins. This area was built much higher up and was either built new from the ground up, or so completely remodeled that it might as well have been.

The skyline was peppered with both pointed and flat-topped buildings much taller than the older ones. Regardless of the style, every building had spacious terraces and balconies outside. I remembered how Ashur had flown perfectly vertically to set my car down. It would be easy enough for them to swoop down to the wide street below. They were very deft fliers, so it made sense to have easy access to the sky everywhere.

A couple of large-winged shapes flew off in the distance, in the sunlight I could truly appreciate the golden-toned scales that made up their hides. They weren't all the exact same color—one was more of a true yellow gold and the other had a little more green in it—but they were both within the gold family. The sun flashed off their sides, giving them a glowing outline as they lazily circled in the air.

Now that I wasn't being chased, I could appreciate the elegance and beauty of them as well as the strength. The long graceful lines, the powerful wings, the sinuous tails and necks. As they rode the air currents without flapping their wings, I understood them to be the silent predators they were.

They inspired equal parts fear and respect. No wonder they were banned from the city domes. I didn't know how humans could stop something that big from destroying everything. It even had me wondering how a bow and arrow was supposed to stand up to a creature like that.

I turned away from the sight when Hathai showed up with two other people. They both looked young, maybe in their late teens, and were dressed in chef's whites. The young woman gave both me and Omari curious glances, but was silent. The boy, too, gave me one long look, and then just focused on setting up the food.

"Thank you," I said to them as they finished and stepped back. "I really appreciate it."

They just nodded and scurried back to the open door. Maybe they were told not to interact with me.

"Give him the oatmeal. It will be easier for him to eat right now," Hathai said.

I nodded. That made sense.

"Come on Omari," I murmured, sliding an arm under his small shoulders and propping him up against me. "You have to eat something."

"Okay," he said, slightly groggy. But he was more alert already.

I carefully spooned oatmeal into his mouth, and he dutifully ate it.

"That doesn't taste very good," he said after half the bowl was finished.

"Do you want something else?"

He shook his head no. Yawning, he snuggled against me. "No, I'm full."

He'd eaten more than half of the creamy-looking oatmeal. Good enough, at least for now. I lowered him back onto the bed and dug into the food myself. I picked out a Danish pastry, biting into it.

Oh, wow. The raspberry at the center of it was the real deal.

We were still able to grow produce in the domes, though everything was carefully regulated to increase efficiency and reduce waste. The water was a constant problem, but filtration systems and underground reserves gave us enough to live on. Of course we had plenty of sun. All of that intensive effort and planning meant produce was expensive.

But here in the dragon stronghold, they'd brought out berries and oatmeal. They must have their own farming set up nearby. I was guessing there was a greenhouse somewhere in the city. Maybe more than one since they weren't hurting for space—growing the grain alone would have taken so much land. They must have their own water sources as well. Transporting heavy containers of water wouldn't be difficult for them considering one dragon could pick up a car.

I imagined dragons going to and fro with giant buckets clutched in their claws. For some reason, the image made me smile.

When I was done eating, Hathai said something into the slim watch on her wrist. The same boy and girl reappeared and took the dishes away.

I sat for a while longer, but restlessness and curiosity had me moving to the railing on one side of the roof, after checking on Omari again.

The city was gorgeous. There was something in the material they used to construct everything that sparkled slightly in the sun, adding dimension to the sandstone colors.

Down on street level, there were plenty of people walking around, going about their day. I saw maybe one car, but everyone else was on foot. With this many people, it looked like they had a fully functioning, bustling economy. I still couldn't get over the reality of this place compared to what I had thought about dragons before encountering them. I didn't know anyone who had ever actually been in a dragon stronghold.

What I learned in school was that dragons and phoenixes showed up after the atmosphere partially burned away and for a while they and humans coexisted together. It all went downhill with Phoenix King Emil. As with many monarchs throughout history, King Emil had been completely off his rocker. But his brand of crazy had been particularly dangerous. He instigated an all-out war with the dragons, proclaiming they were stupid and dangerous beasts that needed to be wiped off the surface of the Earth.

It didn't have much basis in fact, but he'd apparently been a very charismatic leader and had managed to amass enough of a following that he'd been able to put his words into action. He did his best to reach his goal, attempting a full-out genocide. His mistake was assuming dragons were weak.

While dragons were an independent race with self-governed skeins operating in their own territories, nothing united a people more than a common threat. Emil managed to do what the dragons hadn't been able to do for centuries—unite all of them. The attempted genocide quickly turned into total war.

Humans had already polluted the earth to a point that we couldn't come back from but that war did so much damage and resulted in so much loss of life, that it actually slowed down some environmental problems. We would have been in an even worse place now without that bloody conflict. Killing so much of the population—dragons, phoenixes, and humans alike—wasn't the ideal way to achieve it but it was brutally efficient in decreasing our ecological footprint.

The war, combined with the fact that humans needed protection from the sun and from the radiated air while the dragons and phoenixes didn't, naturally resulted in all three groups separating. Dragons and phoenixes still had spats from time to time, but the humans were left out of it. They'd ensured they would be by banning the other two races from the city domes.

Some shouting from the street level drew my eyes to where the commotion was coming from. What was going on? A crowd was gathering, and I moved down the railing to get a better look. I was so engrossed in trying to figure out what was happening down there that I almost bumped right into a guard.

"Oops. Sorry."

His face was surprisingly young this close. Frowning, he leaned towards me, inhaling. What was with these people? I'd showered only a few hours ago.

"That's enough, Ivan," said a familiar voice.

Ashur strode out from the rooftop access door, his eyes on the guard. The sun sparkled in the light parts of his hair, highlighted his high cheekbones, and glinted off his skin. The parts that caught the sun looked like molten gold. I stared, caught by the almost otherworldly beauty of him.

This was someone who belonged in the sun.

Today, he was dressed in a fitted white t-shirt that contrasted with his golden-brown skin and a pair of ripped jeans. Not stylish and deliberately created for fashion either, the pants were just old and worn in.

His attention wasn't on me. He was giving the guard a hard look. The young man moved back to his proper pose, completely at attention once again.

Then Ashur's piercing eyes moved over to me and I was subject to the full force of the Dragon Lord's attention. Intimidating, yes. It really wasn't fair that anyone could have so much sex appeal.

His eyes left mine for a moment to look over to where Omari was lying in one of the beds.

"Keeping watch? Do you think we would hurt a child?" he asked, his eyes turning back to me, his jaw tight. "We aren't animals."

I refused to be made wrong for my caution. "Well, we're not exactly here of our own volition," I pointed out, crossing my arms. "And I'm responsible for his safety."

He looked away from me and over to the tops of the buildings, his eyes tracking the two dragons I was watching earlier.

"I give you my word that we won't hurt him. He's safe here."

I looked back over at Omari and Hathai, who was watching him. I'd taken her for a complete hard-ass, but even I could see that her face had softened as she stood next to the kid.

"I need to speak to you. Would you be comfortable if we just went to the other side of the roof?" Ashur asked.

I sighed, nodding. If something happened, I wouldn't be too far. "Lead the way."

He led us all the way to the other end of the railing. He leaned against it like he had last night, bracing his forearms.

I took up a spot next to him warily. "What did you want to talk to me about?" I asked.

He looked down at the streets, one wrist loosely clasped in his other hand. After a beat of silence, he looked over at me, his eyes scanning my exposed skin. I really wished I'd taken the time to get dressed. My mind hadn't been on myself at all because of Omari's condition this morning and I was still in the tank top and loose bottoms I'd worn to sleep last night.

"I want to talk about you." That didn't sound good. His next question confirmed that thought. "Mia—do you know who your parents are?"

My heart gave a hard thump inside my chest.

CHAPTER ELEVEN

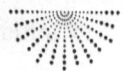

$\mathcal{M}$y eyes were locked on the side of his face as he turned back to the street below.

Nothing changed outwardly, but it was like I was standing completely naked. My heartbeat was fast, my mouth was dry, and I was frozen in place.

"That's none of your business," I finally said. "And no, you can't argue that it is this time."

He shrugged and turned to me, his blue eyes calm and watchful. "You've never been around dragons before, have you?" he asked after a moment.

I stayed silent.

"I can smell it on you, you know." His eyes scanned my face. "I knew even before you came out into the sun."

I swallowed, unable to look away from his direct gaze. "Smell what?"

"That you're not human." He frowned at me a little. "Or at least not all human."

He could smell it on me? No wonder everyone had been sniffing at me so weirdly. I had no idea a dragon's sense of smell was so acute. Spending my entire life in the city dome had left me at a real disadvantage. No wonder my mom didn't want me leaving.

I was so worried about my skin giving me away, I hadn't even considered my scent. I looked down at my arm. I had a rose-gold sheen to my skin, though it wasn't nearly as apparent as Ashur's golden shine. At certain angles, he looked like he was made of the warm metal.

"You didn't know I could smell it on you?" he asked curiously.

"No." There was no point in denying it now.

"So, was it your mother or your father who was phoenix? And which side was dragon?"

I must have misheard him. "What?"

He straightened, keeping one hand on the railing. "Which side was which?"

"I...I'm part dragon. My mother was mixed. But I'm not phoenix." I'd always assumed my father must also have been at least part dragon.

Ashur took a step towards me. I stood completely still as he leaned in and took in another breath, this time close to my neck. When he exhaled, his hot breath sent tingles down my spine. My hands clenched into fists. He finally straightened, shaking his head.

"I'm not mistaken," he said confidently, watching my face. "You're also part phoenix." He took my wrist in hand and stretched my arm out, the contact sending a jolt through me. "Just look at your skin if you don't believe me. It isn't gold like a dragon or copper like a phoenix, but a shade somewhere in between. The shine is dimmer due to the human aspect, but the tone is unmistakable."

I shook my head, pulling my arm away from the callused heat of his hand and looking away from him to the city, though I wasn't really seeing anything.

"That's not possible," I said, even as doubt seeped in. "My

mom would have told me. And I know phoenixes and dragons can't stand each other."

He watched me, thoughts running through his eyes. "True enough. But do you really believe intermingling has never happened? We didn't always used to be so separated. And in the end, we're all just people." I didn't know how to answer that. "Where is your mother now?" he continued.

I swallowed, tightness in my eyes and my throat. It would be really nice to have her to talk to right now. Someone I could confide in.

"She's dead," I said. An awkward pause followed, one I was familiar with since childhood.

"I'm sorry," Ashur offered, his voice softer now.

I shrugged. "It's been a long time." I liked to say that when people heard about my mother. Even though the truth was, it still seemed like yesterday. I didn't want to betray that vulnerability if I could help it.

"Maybe she was waiting to tell you until you grew older," he suggested gently.

"Hmmm." Mom never answered any of my questions. I didn't know if age would have changed that about her. But I was stronger and more assertive now. Maybe it would have made a difference. Not that I would ever know.

"Look," he continued, reaching out to touch my arm again lightly. "I'm not bringing this up for no reason. Your scent is very unusual. Any dragon and any phoenix, if they get close enough to you, will pick up on the fact that you're part phoenix, dragon, and human. I know I don't have to tell you how rare that is. The fact that you have such a significant amount of all three that I could scent them so clearly, means that you can't hide it. Not out here. Maybe among humans who can't smell worth shit," he added with a touch of derision.

"Watch it," I said mildly, though I wasn't really offended. "I'm part human too."

His lips tilted in a small smile. But it faded as he regarded me. "The only reason I'm bringing this up is because you're planning on taking that child to phoenix territory. Is that a good idea?"

I sighed. Not really. "It doesn't matter if it's a good idea. It's the job I accepted and the job I have to carry out."

He stared, his face stoic. "You shouldn't have taken the job."

"I didn't have a choice."

"Of course you did."

I didn't owe him an explanation. But maybe this was part of the reason he was keeping us here. "I have to take Omari to phoenix territory. His family is there."

"Are they?" he countered. "If they cared so much, why isn't he with them already? Why did he end up with you? I'm assuming you were in the city dome directly south of here, correct?"

I nodded. That wasn't a secret.

He continued. "I know you were trying to drive through our territory at night to avoid contact, so you had some reason to be wary of dragons. I'm not saying that instinct was wrong." He paused for a long moment, his eyes far away, looking over the city to the horizon. "Do you know anything about phoenixes? Because they're much worse than dragons. Harsher. Especially their king." His mouth tightened. "It must run in their line, that thread of cruelty."

I frowned. "Harsher in what way?"

"In every way," he said, his face grim. "Harsher with their children, much harsher with outsiders. The idea of purity that started the war didn't disappear after it ended. If you'd attempted to travel through phoenix territory like you did mine, they wouldn't have hesitated at seeing the child. They would've killed you on sight."

I had the urge to point out that that was exactly what I'd feared would happen in his territory. Maybe his own suspicion was unfounded. But I shouldn't mention that. Hey, maybe as I got older I was actually learning how to watch my tongue.

"Are you sure you're not biased?" Or maybe not.

His face hardened. "You can choose to believe me or not," he said, his expression more distant now. "I have no reason to lie to you. And this isn't anything beyond a friendly warning."

"Consider me warned," I returned just as coolly.

He nodded once and stepped away. I watched his back as he disappeared through the door then I turned back to the view. Way to alienate the one person whose mercy we were at right now. Real smart move. In my defense, he'd completely blindsided me with this conversation, and it had left me uncomfortable and unsettled. What did any of this mean? Did it change anything really?

If I was part dragon or part phoenix, or both, that didn't change the fact that I was probably safest in the city dome where I didn't have a lot of interaction with either. Especially now that I knew both phoenixes and dragons would know that I was partially their blood just by scent. I was under no illusions that my mother was living in a city dome among humans because that was what she wanted in life. There was no other reason for us to be there other than for protection.

If what Ashur said about the phoenixes was accurate, should I take Omari there? Why would I be hired to transport him if there wasn't someone there who wanted him, who cared about him?

This wasn't a job I'd sought out, but now it was more than a job. I was involved way beyond a professional level. If I didn't take Omari to the final destination, Santiago would be sure to rat me out. However, if it was between protecting myself or Omari, there wasn't a contest. For better or worse, I was in charge of his safety. He couldn't protect himself yet.

I shook my head, bending over to rest my head in my hands, bracing my elbows on the railing. Somehow, this had turned into an even-more-complicated mess than it already was.

"Mia?"

I turned at Omari's voice to find him sitting up in bed, looking for me.

"I'm right here," I called out, hurrying over to him. His relieved smile when he saw me pulled at my heart in a way nothing really had for a long time. For good or bad, I was well and truly emotionally invested.

As I sat down next to Omari and hugged him back when he reached for me, I was more conflicted than ever.

What should I do?

What was the right thing to do?

CHAPTER TWELVE

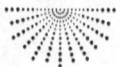

"*A*nd then Cara changed and showed me her dragon form! She was this big!" Omari stretched his arms out as far as they could go and looked at them. "Even bigger than this!"

I laughed, transferring more fruit to his plate. "Eat the strawberries," I said.

He lowered his arms and happily stuffed his face. He was looking much better than he had just a couple of days ago. The gray tinge to his skin was gone and he had more energy than ever. He didn't lag anymore when the sun went down, either.

He was still spending most of his days up on the roof soaking in the sun, which Hathai had suggested—turned out she was a nurse who had some experience with children. It might have been why she'd been assigned to us in the first place. Some of the dragon children had started venturing out on the roof now, curious about who was up there. The guards were still very careful, staying close to us when their own children came near Omari or me. Not that I blamed them.

Omari had blossomed under the attention of the handful of children brave enough to wander up to him. At first, I was afraid they would be unkind, but they weren't. They were sure to include Omari in their games. Then I was afraid they'd change and fly off, leaving Omari out, but then I found out that dragons were only able to really fly after they turned eight. The young kids could glide if they jumped off the building and landed safely, but they weren't yet strong enough to lift themselves using only the power of their wings.

In the last day or so, Cara had emerged as his favorite. All the kids would come up to the roof and play together, but Omari tended to stay next to his new friend. I was glad he was doing better, but I wasn't sure about the emerging friendships. I was happy that he had children to play with, but the longer we stayed, the harder it would be for him to leave.

I hadn't pushed about leaving yet because I was worried about Omari. Tomorrow or the next day, he would be in good enough health to travel again. And then I would have a decision to make.

Someone hired Santiago to find a way to get Omari back to phoenix territory. So, logically, he must have a family who wanted him. Or maybe the phoenixes were just good about looking after their own kind.

But Ashur was also right about the fact that Omari was in the city dome for a reason. Why would someone have brought him there unless they were trying to protect him? That was exactly why my own mother brought me to the dome to live among the humans. She thought it would be safer to stay out of contact with dragons and phoenixes.

Our lives there hadn't been easy, and mine wasn't now. I had to be careful always, had to hide parts of myself to make sure that I wasn't discovered. Had to lie to everyone, even the people closest to me.

It was one of the reasons why I didn't have friends.

When I was younger, I would make them, but I wasn't much of a joiner to begin with. Having to keep such a large secret made it difficult to maintain friendships. On top of that, my mom didn't really encourage those kinds of connections. I understood as I grew older.

The more close friends I had, the more likely I was to reveal who I was to them.

And mom always told me the only person you could trust with yourself was yourself. As I got older and more experienced, I understood why she had come to such a hard conclusion about people in general. And despite that care and sacrifice, I was still found out.

No, life in the city dome wouldn't be easy for Omari either. He would have to learn to be more closed off, to be more careful. To be less himself. Didn't I owe him a chance to be himself? Didn't I owe it to him to at least go and see if it was the place for him?

He was too young to really know what it was like to not truly belonging anywhere. Even when I thought I was just part dragon and human, I didn't belong among either group. Now that I knew I was also part phoenix, I was somehow even more isolated. Part of everyone but belonging to no one.

I responded to Omari's happy chatter while he ate, but the whole time I worried, wondering what the best course of action was. My thoughts and Omari's stream of consciousness were both interrupted by a knock at the door. Raising my eyebrows, I stood up to open it.

Who would be knocking on our door right now?

I opened it and looked out, not seeing anybody.

"Hello," came from a few feet below my eye level. I

looked down into Cara's big brown eyes, a cute bob high-lighting the roundness of her cheeks. Today, she was dressed in a bright yellow pair of shorts, a pink t-shirt with a cheery yellow sun and white sneakers with yellow laces on her tiny feet.

"Hello," I said, smiling at her.

She twisted her hands behind herself and shuffled her feet. "Can Omari come out to play?" she asked hopefully.

"Can I?"

Light running steps behind me were almost muted by the carpet as Omari hurried to the door. "Hi Cara! Can I go out and play?" he asked again, his eyes big as he looked up at me.

I look back and forth between the two large pairs of hopeful eyes. Cuteness overload. I smiled, shaking my head. I didn't stand a chance.

"All right."

He let out a whoop and ran out into the hall with Cara. "Make sure you stay out in the sun! Take your shirt off!"

"I will!" he yelled over his shoulder as they ran to the elevators.

Laughing to myself, I closed the door and sat down on the couch.

Without Omari in the room, quiet settled around me. I was really alone. Was I already getting used to having him around? Used to having his chatter fill the space around me, his quick smile, his enthusiastic bear hugs? If so, I was being very stupid. He wasn't mine to keep. And my life wasn't meant for a child anyway.

Maybe it never would be.

Sighing, I stood up.

I could just sit in the room and mope, feeling sorry for myself. Or I could go outside. Maybe to the car my employer had so graciously provided. All my stuff was still in there. The clean pair of sweats and the t-shirt I had on were courtesy of the guest clothing in the closet, but it would be nice to have my own things.

Maybe I could do some reconnaissance while I was out there.

I slipped my feet into my boots and left the room, closing the door behind me. The carpet sank under my feet as I traced the same path the children had just taken. As I looked around, I still couldn't get over how much money was spent on this building. The sconces, the carpeting, the paintings, the wallpaper—even the air freshener smelled expensive. Some kind of citrus and herb mix.

I stopped at a painting of a lush forest that I passed every day. A river flowed through the center, with the sun sparkling on it. I took a step closer to get a better look. The variations of green, from dark and rich to light and bright, the white edges of the water that indicated rushing motion, the clear blue of the sky... It was beautiful. It made me want to step right into the painting and revel in my surroundings.

But nothing like that was left on Earth anymore. Not after all we had done to it.

I stood and admired the beauty that once was, keenly aware of the loss of it. Shaking my head, I stepped away. Dreaming of what could have been was no use. It was one of the mottos I lived by.

Life was too painful otherwise.

When I reached the elevator, Enzi stepped up smoothly next to me. I had wondered where he'd gone. There had been a guard on me the whole time I had been here. I would do the same in their shoes. Not that I had my own palace where I could invite strange guests...err, well prisoners to stay. Though that would be pretty awesome.

"Hey," I greeted him as I stepped into the elevator.

He followed me in. "Hello. Where are you off to?" he asked nonchalantly, but his eyes were sharp.

I pressed the button for the first floor.

"I want to go take a look at my car," I said. "Is that okay?"

He hesitated but then nodded. "That's fine. I just have to come with you."

Fair enough. We were silent as we descended.

"Omari seems to be adjusting well," Enzi commented.

I nodded. "Yes." I looked over at him. "It isn't a problem that he's playing with other kids, is it?"

"No," he said. "He's just a child. And if it were a problem, we wouldn't have let them up on the roof in the first place."

True. And they also had an eye on the children the whole time to make sure nothing bad happened. I'd noticed the discreet tail before.

The doors opened into the front lobby, and again the detailed carvings and the chandelier drew my admiring eyes. As we walked through it, I wondered what it was like to grow up like this. Wealthy. Powerful. Secure.

"Was Ashur's father the Dragon Lord before him?" I asked as our footsteps echoed through the large room.

There were people hanging around now because it was daytime, and I could see the sideways glances they sent my way. I stared back and they looked away. I had the sudden urge to say boo.

"No," Enzi said. "Do you think we're a monarchy?" he asked, sounding offended.

I shrugged. "I don't know what you are," I said honestly. "It isn't like we're taught much about Phoenix and Dragon political structures in the city domes."

"You aren't? But that's ridiculous! We're taught about human culture and city dome politics in elementary school."

"Well, I don't know what to tell you. We mostly just get a dose of how dangerous you are and why we need to be separated from you."

He shook his head, looking irritated. "Figures," he muttered. "Humans."

We stepped onto the bustling street. It wasn't nearly as crowded as I was used to streets being in the dome. The fact that there was basically no automobile traffic helped. Other than the wideness of the streets and the slightly different styles people wore—more loose and light colors, which made sense in the desert—I could've been in the city dome. Well, except for the fact that the sun was beating down on us.

"I don't have any idea where I'm going, by the way," I admitted. "Feel free to lead the way."

Enzi chuckled and took a step in front of me. "Your car was moved to one of the garages," he explained. He walked me down a block and then turned into what looked like a standard parking garage. I guess there wasn't really any better way to store cars.

I was surprised to find ones I recognized, familiar makes and models, along with more exotic ones. Enzi saw me looking.

"Ashur likes cars," he explained as he led me to the back corner. "There's a level of just motorcycles too."

"Must be nice to be the Dragon Lord," I muttered.

"It is," Enzi agreed. "But he works his ass off for it. He's the reason why our skein is doing so well in the first place. He has a head for business and the strength to keep everyone in line, keep everything stable."

"Keep everybody in line?" I asked.

"Yes." He frowned. "Dragons and phoenixes both have very territorial urges. If we didn't have someone strong at the helm, our instinct would be to overthrow him. So, even though our Dragon Lord is chosen through a consensus, there's a chance he won't stay in the position if he isn't strong enough."

I blinked. "Must make elections pretty exciting," I said finally.

He grinned. "You have no idea."

We reached the small tank that was my car and Enzi opened the driver's side door for me. "Sweet ride, by the way," he commented as I crawled inside.

"Thanks. It's just a loaner," I clarified.

"Ah."

I grabbed my bag and my eyes fell on my bows. They might take it as a sign of aggression if I just carried them around, but... I took them as well. I figured Enzi would tell me if I couldn't bring them up. I left the extra knives, but I took the sword. I wouldn't reasonably be able to fight my way out if I had to, but having a few more weapons would make me feel better.

When I stepped back out, Enzi's eyebrows went up.

"Planning on murdering us in our sleep on your way out?" he asked dryly.

I shook my head. "I know I wouldn't make it," I said honestly.

I now knew exactly how secure they kept the perimeter. Even if Omari hadn't screamed, I was sure they'd have known we were there anyway by the time we hit the city. Maybe the people Jacob had heard about succeeding had gone through territories where the dragons weren't as vigilant.

Enzi nodded. "You wouldn't," he agreed. "But I don't know if Ashur is going to be okay with you having that much weaponry inside."

I sighed. I tried.

"It was worth a shot," he said, echoing my thoughts with a grin. "Where should I–"

A blaring alarm sounded, interrupting what he was going

to say. I winced, covering one ear with my shoulder because my hands were full.

"What's that?" I yelled over the racket.

Enzi's face was grim. "We're being attacked!"

That's when the screams started. And the roars.

Cursing, Enzi turned and ran back the way we'd come from, straight to the street. I ducked into the car and strapped the extra knives and my sword to myself. Then I grabbed only the compound bow I used for long distances, along with my quiver.

But then I hesitated. It wasn't really my place to help them defend against anyone. And this was a perfect distraction. I could grab Omari and run, take him to the phoenix territory. But first I needed to find him. I ran out the way we'd come in, Enzi already long gone. When I reached the street exit, I slowed down and looked out.

People were running in all directions, seeking shelter in the buildings, clutching children, older people. Trying to get the noncombatants out of the way.

Hathai ran down the street, her face grim, her attention on the sky above. She crouched down and burst into her dragon form, a beautiful matte gold with a darker ring around her neck. She launched herself off the street in a powerful surge, her wings flapping hard enough that the gust of wind pushed me back.

I chanced a look up.

The air was filled with dragons, the golden-hued ones that I was used to seeing, but also ones with lavender-tinted scales, their mouths open as they shot fire.

I watched as one of the attacking dragons made a beeline for Hathai, breathing fire as it flew. It clawed at her wings with its talons before she'd had a chance to fully get her bearings.

My heart was in my throat as I watched. Come on, Hathai.

She tore herself free, leaving small rents in her wings, firing back just as harshly as she rose in the sky. But she was hurt, her wings a little off from the tears. It was clear the moment she decided she wasn't going down alone.

I held my breath as Hathai angled her body and shot right at the dragon who'd attacked her. They slammed onto the street in front of me, the ground cracking underneath from the impact. Hathai was on top of the purple one, both of them clawing and biting at each other.

They were occupied. I could run right past, back to Ashur's building where Omari was.

The lavender one lurched and rolled, shoving the golden one underneath it.

Shit.

I hesitated for another moment. I remembered Hathai watching over Omari, her face soft.

"Fuck," I muttered.

I pulled out my release and looped it over my hand. I took one of the arrows out of my quiver. They were formed to puncture the thick hides of dragons and cut through phoenix plumage. I'd never used them to do that, but I practiced constantly.

Something about focusing on a target and trying to hit it was always calming to me. Even now, as I nocked the arrow, clicked it into place, and pulled back on the string, my eye focused on the sights and my heart beat slowed, my breathing evening out.

Stilling my body, I aimed. I didn't know how well these arrows worked on an actual dragon so I needed to aim at a vulnerable spot. The eye was a good bet.

I waited until the lavender dragon reared back, opening its mouth to bite. Got it. I tapped the release.

The purple dragon's eye sprouted an arrow.

Bull's-eye.

It went limp almost immediately. The arrow was embedded in the brain. It may not have been dead, but it was definitely incapacitated.

My stomach rolled but I pushed past it. This wasn't a game. They were the ones that had attacked.

Hathai looked over at me and nodded her large head in acknowledgment. Then she launched herself into the air to rejoin the fight in the sky, wings apparently judged good enough.

I needed a better vantage point. I ran down the street, hugging the side of the building as closely as I could. I hoped I wouldn't be fried before I got back to Ashur's. I ducked as another dragon fell into the building across from me, crumbling the front of it with the impact. Its golden scales glimmered as it struggled to rise from the rubble.

The smart thing to do would have been to take cover and wait this out. It was too dangerous to drive the car out. The dragons would have gotten Omari to a safe place. I wasn't going to be able to change the tide of this fight.

I kept moving. This may have been one of the stupidest things that I'd ever done. Though the last week or so had certainly been a doozy. There were so many stupid things to choose from.

I winced as a tunnel of flame engulfed the dragon that had hit the building.

It was so hot that it almost singed me from this far away. The yellow and orange of the fluid-like stream of fire was fascinating. Dragons were resistant to heat, but not to such a direct flame for such a prolonged period of time. Just like the armor on the car.

But the only way to get a good shot at the dragon who was burning the golden one was to walk out into the street.

Out into the open.

Nope. I wasn't that stupid.

I watched my own feet as they turned and walked out into the street.

Okay. Maybe I was.

CHAPTER THIRTEEN

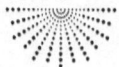

I turned in the direction the tunnel of flame was originating from as I neared the center of the street. The heat from the fire was hot enough to parch my face and dry my eyes even from yards away.

I looked up to see a lavender-hued dragon in the air, its wings flapping as it hovered in place, its jaws agape as the fire rushed out.

I just stared in awe for a few seconds.

I'd seen the dragons fly and there was something in their size and the clear power in their bodies that inspired respect. But to witness it as heat from the flames licked my skin, the sizzle of burning flesh hot in my nose...

Yup. Fear. But I didn't have time for it. I needed to work fast if I was going to be of any real help.

Bracing my feet, I brought my bow up and took a deep breath, calming my heart. The angle was too weird, I didn't have a clear shot at its eyes. Shooting for it anyway might do nothing, or distract it and make it attack me.

Not great outcomes. But I couldn't just do nothing.

I scanned its body quickly and finally decided on a shot I

might be able to make. Adjusting the bow, I aimed at the place where its wing joined with its shoulder. I might be able to incapacitate it, forcing it to drop to the ground.

No time for second guesses. I tapped the release.

Just as the arrow flew, a gust of wind from another pair of approaching wings changed the trajectory. It just missed what I was aiming for, and instead lodged right in the dragon's shoulder.

Well, shit.

The column of flame abruptly disappeared.

Yellow eyes turned to look at me. And they weren't happy.

I turned as the sound of another pair of wings drew closer. It was another purple dragon. It stopped, hovering to my left, not nearly far enough away for my comfort. Though far enough would probably be on the other side of the city, maybe the planet.

Double shit. This was it. At least death by dragon sounded badass. Not that anyone but dragons would know.

Then a bright gold flash hit my peripheral vision. My gaze jerked back over to the dragon that I'd managed to annoy just in time to see the golden dragon hit it from the side, pushing it away.

Away from me.

I recognized that bright gold flash, though I didn't know how when he was going so fast. But I knew it was him. Ashur.

I turned back to the other dragon still hovering near me. Why wasn't I dead? One quick burst of flame and I'd be gone. Mia kabob.

My eyes caught its deep yellow ones as it twisted its neck, its head tilting to the side and the slits of its nostrils flaring. It drew even closer, and then landed just yards from me. My hands itched to draw my bow, but that might set it off.

Did dragons eat people? Now probably wasn't the best time to speculate on that particular topic.

I took some slow steps back.

It raised its head, straightening it again, as it regarded me.

I frowned, completely confused. What was going on?

The strange stare-down lasted for a few more seconds, though it seemed much longer. Time had a certain elasticity to it when adrenaline was pumping that hard.

A loud roar from above us was what finally broke it. The dragon's attention immediately veered upwards. With one last look at me, it beat its wings and propelled itself off the street. Its neck stretched upwards as it rose, revealing a distinctive star-shaped darker patch on its chest.

I stood, taking deep breaths as I tried to get my body back under control. I opened my hands, stretching them out. I was still alive. Somehow.

I didn't know what had just happened, but I didn't have time to dwell on it.

The golden dragon that was still huddled in the building right next to me moved, pieces of the building rolling down onto the street. I took a step back, looking up. It pushed away from the building, half of its body almost black from the fire, the other half still intact. Visibly anyway. Miraculously, its wings were still perfectly fine, probably protected by the way the building had wrapped around them.

It shook its head, getting its bearings, and also launched itself back into the air to rejoin the fight. Couldn't fault his or her commitment.

But I really needed to move. Now.

Getting myself back into gear, I hurried down the street to Ashur's building. The harsh sounds of the battle continued up above me, but I kept my head down and stayed as close to the buildings as I could.

It was difficult not to look up at the mash-up of loud

sounds: the flapping of wings, the crackle of fire, the pain and rage filled roars. Thankfully, the battle stayed in the air for the rest of the way.

When I reached Ashur's building, I ran up the steps. The doors were closed. I tried them.

Locked.

I pounded on them, but the thick, sturdy barrier didn't move at all. And nobody answered.

"Fuck."

I took a few steps back and looked up the building in frustration.

I wasn't helping anybody down here. I racked my brain for another solution, and remembered something from when I first arrived here. It wasn't ideal, but this wasn't exactly an ideal situation.

I circled the building, my eyes scanning the walls. And I found it—the sun shone down, glinting off the ladder. It looked ridiculously flimsy as it traveled up the side of the place. I traced it with my eyes, all the way up the dizzying length of the building.

Maybe now was the time to mention that I'd never been the biggest fan of heights.

I might even be an active hater of them.

Though I'd been forced to get over the worst of it over the years. I could do fire escapes, stairs, or even a nice, stable rooftop. A ladder didn't have quite the same sturdiness.

It was a long way up. But also the only way up.

Silently cursing in an effort to release some of my nervous energy, I secured the bow and quiver on my back to free my hands. I gripped the hot metal but immediately let go, the heat from it almost burning my hands even from that brief touch. I had some resistance to heat, but maybe pure dragons had more.

I patted my pockets, hoping I had them on me-- aha. I

pulled out my insulated, fingerless gloves. I shoved my hands into them and tried to touch the ladder again. It still wasn't comfortable, but my palms weren't burning. I'd make do.

I kept my eyes on the building in front of me as I started climbing. I just needed to keep moving.

Hand.

Foot.

Push up.

I focused on each individual movement, trying not to think about the fact that I was moving vertically. With nothing to catch me if I fell.

As I rose higher, the wind picked up. The heat from multiple streams of fire mixed with the already-hot sun, as if the anxiety and adrenaline weren't enough to make me sweat already. I wiped my face with my arm before the sweat started stinging my eyes.

I was maybe three-quarters of the way up when something swooped past me so fast, I almost lost my grip. I let out a huff of breath and hugged the ladder.

My heart had skipped a beat and then gone crazy.

All right. Still alive. Taking a deep breath, I turned to look. But as I moved my head, my eyes fell on the world beneath me.

Oh man. The street look like a narrow strip below. I was a long way up.

A dizzy spell hit me and jerked my eyes back up. Fainting now was not the way to go. Picturing falling and becoming a pancake was not helpful either.

Not at all.

Forcing myself to look where the dragon who'd swooped by had gone, I found the bright gold of Ashur's hide. And the three cool-colored dragons surrounding him. As I focused on them, they attacked with fire and claws and teeth.

Ashur dodged and maneuvered his large body expertly,

but there was no way he was going to be able to keep them off him. Not with all three attacking at once. I couldn't just sit back and let them take him down.

It was a much stronger reaction than I'd had to Hathai. I really didn't want to examine why that was.

I glanced back up to see how much farther I had to go before I reached the roof. It would take me too long.

"Wonderful," I muttered to myself as I hooked an arm around a rung and pulled my bow off my back. "Just what I wanted to do. Hang precariously from a great height while in the middle of a war zone."

I wrapped one of my legs around the side of the ladder for good measure and pulled an arrow out of my quiver. I couldn't focus on the height right now. I needed to aim. So I aimed. I cut out any thoughts about how high I was and raised my bow as I watched for an opening.

Ashur pushed one of them away with a roar, and it went tumbling through the air only to catch itself with a hard pump of its wings.

Bingo.

I took a deep breath and stilled myself. The air currents were unpredictable with so many wings in the air. I adjusted as well as I could and tapped the release. My arrow veered too far to the left and instead embedded itself shallowly in the dragon's snout.

It roared and swung its head over to look at me. Not again.

I quickly got another arrow and brought my bow up as the irritated dragon tucked its wings close to its body and darted in my direction, cutting through the air fast. My heart was pounding in my chest but I forced that sensation away. I'd only have one shot at this. My eyes zeroed in on one of the narrowed eyes.

If I waited too long, it could slam into me. If I didn't wait long enough, my shot might not hit my target or it might not penetrate enough to be effective. Both would be disastrous.

My finger itched to hit the trigger. Wait for it. Wait for it...

There.

I released the arrow.

It grew from the dragon's right eye, buried halfway in.

Yes!

I watched its other eye glaze over as death came for it.

But it was already plummeting in my direction. It wasn't alive anymore to stop itself short before impact. I scrambled up the ladder, trying to move as quickly as I could without slipping. Don't think about falling!

The dragon slammed into the building right underneath me and I hung onto the ladder for dear life as it shook. If the ladder tore off the building, it wouldn't matter how tightly I was hanging on. I was trying really hard not to think about that either as I waited to see what would happen.

I opened my eyes when the shaking finally subsided. Still on the building. Okay. That was good. I looked down. The dragon was half embedded into the side of the building, its hindquarters and tail the only parts still visible. Not very dignified, but you couldn't win them all.

I took a moment to get my breathing back under control, closing my eyes again. Okay, I had this. No problem. I forced my muscles to unclench and opened my eyes to look up.

With the odds a little more even, Ashur had already dispatched one of the other dragons and the last one looked like it wasn't going to be able to dodge him for much longer. But I'd drawn more attention with my shot than I'd realized. A slightly darker mauve dragon was headed right at me, its eyes locked on my body. I could not be stuck on this ladder for another attack. I'd already reached my quota of heart attacks, thanks. I needed to get to the top.

An incoming dragon was apparently enough motivation to get me going quickly. After this was over, I was going to kiss the ground. I wrapped up the rest of the distance at record speed.

No time, no time.

I rolled over the short wall at the top and turned, bringing my bow up with the same movement. But I was too late. It was like I had all the time in the world and none at all.

I watched the dragon's jaws inch open, revealing the crimson interior of its mouth, its glistening fangs. At the very back of its throat was a tiny flicker of flame.

And I watched as it grew bigger.

Bigger.

The heat hit me first. Before the flames ever touched me, the heat seared my skin and burned my hair. It smelled awful.

There was no time to do anything. The flame engulfed me, a bright yellow tinged with orange red. The pain was excruciating. An all-encompassing, inescapable pain like nothing I'd ever experienced before.

I thought I saw another flash of lavender, a distinct star shape. I vaguely realized it was the dragon from earlier as it knocked my attacker aside. But I must have been delirious.

Why would it do that?

I fell to my knees, my body completely not under my control. I was numb. I knew I was hurt. Badly.

The glint of familiar gold and a roar of pure rage. A bright gold shape and the deeper purple that had just been knocked aside collided.

Was that Ashur?

I listed over to the side, and my body hit the floor. The impact wracked me in pain, but in a distant, disconnected way.

And then I knew nothing.

CHAPTER FOURTEEN

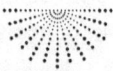

I dreamed of pain. And shouting. And multiple voices, all talking at once.

Then one particularly deep voice. One that was becoming familiar.

"Stay with me Mia. I decide whether or not you can leave, remember?" he demanded in a grim voice.

Then I just drifted. In the darkness. I sank into it gratefully, sensing that coming out of it would not be good. There wasn't anything waiting for me. But I couldn't drift in the cool, soothing darkness forever, no matter how much I wanted to. I started drawing closer and closer to wakefulness. I didn't know how much time passed before I actually opened my eyes again.

Something was wrong. I couldn't see. Everything was blurry, dim. All I could make out was white. I tried to get up. A wave of debilitating pain hit me. I froze. Okay, moving wasn't a great idea.

I sucked in a breath.

There was a vague rustling next to me and in a few

minutes, the pain drifted away again, behind an odd, foggy wall.

"Mia?" It was Ashur. His voice didn't sound right though.

"Yes," I tried to say, but it came out as a hoarse, unrecognizable sound. What was wrong with me?

I started to move again, but then remembered the pain.

"Stay still Mia," Ashur's voice again, oddly gentle. Ragged. "You're hurt."

Hurt? "What...?"

"You were burned," he responded. "You've been in the med unit for a few days now." He paused. "You're healing too slowly."

Burned?

A jumble of images started flashing in my brain. The fighting. The harrowing climb up the ladder. The darker purple dragon coming right at me.

I swallowed. Burns were bad.

I was guessing burns from a dragon weren't any different. I didn't really want to know how damaged I was, like not knowing meant it hadn't actually happened. But I've always tried not to run from reality.

"How bad?" I asked. At least the drugs were helping. My anxiety and fear were a bit muffled under whatever it was they'd given me.

The silence made the kernel of fear inside me grow bigger though.

"Bad," he finally admitted, softly.

I swallowed. That hesitation spoke for itself, didn't it? I found I wasn't quite ready to acknowledge that yet, no matter how much I usually liked to face problems head on.

"Omari?" I asked.

"He's fine. He was kept safe along with the other children."

"Can I see him?" I guess that wasn't the right choice of words considering I couldn't really see anything.

A short silence once again. Not great. My suspicion was confirmed when he answered.

"We've been keeping him away because..." he trailed off. His throat clicked as he swallowed. He tried again. "He wants to see you, but we didn't think it was a good idea until you were better."

I knew what he was saying. They didn't want to unnecessarily traumatize a child. I was glad they hadn't let him see me if it was really that bad. I was going to have to face that head-on soon enough.

"Why did they attack?" I asked instead.

"Cinira's violet skein has an old grudge against us that she makes sure to keep alive. We usually just give them a wide berth to keep the peace. From what I can gather, someone from their skein went missing. And they thought we might be to blame."

"Why would they think that?"

"That's a story too long to get into right now."

I opened my mouth to speak again, but coughed, the metallic taste of blood coating my tongue.

"Here," Ashur said softly, bringing a cup of water to my lips.

The cool liquid eased my raw throat a little but not enough.

"Were you to blame?" I asked. "For the missing person?"

"No," he said shortly.

I believed him. He wasn't the type of person to lie about that just for his own ends. Maybe trusting him wasn't the smartest thing ever, but he hadn't given me a reason to doubt him yet.

"You're healing with almost human slowness," he explained. "I've been waiting here for you to wake up."

"Why?" I was going to be just as hurt awake or asleep.

"Because you need to change," he said patiently.

"What?"

"You need to change into your other form. The change helps us heal. Cells are renewed because they have to turn over." The air moved around me. His voice was closer as he continued. "The burns are bad, Mia. But a full change to your other form and back should heal them."

I shook my head, but stopped as it set off another cascade of pain. I really needed to be more careful of movement. I breathed through it while Ashur waited quietly.

"I can't," I finally said. "I can't change."

"You can," he argued. "You have to."

"Wouldn't I have changed already if I could? It's never happened!" I argued, too scared to latch onto the hope he was giving me, slim as it was.

"Did anyone ever show you how?" he pointed out. "It isn't like it just happens one day, not for someone like you who didn't grow up around people like yourself."

I shook my head, trying desperately to squash the hope that kept trying to rise up inside me.

"I can't," I insisted. "According to you, I'm not a dragon or phoenix, not completely. And there's human banging around inside me too. How could I transform into anything if all of that is competing? If it's all jumbled together?"

He paused as he considered that. "You're more phoenix and dragon than human," he said in a quiet voice. "Which means more of you can change than not. You have to try." The sound of him shifting in his seat. "You have to. For Omari's sake."

"Cheap shot," I remarked sharply.

"I'll use any shot I have to get you to at least try," he said, completely unrepentant. "You're being stubborn for no reason right now."

I sighed and tried really hard not to move anything.

"What do you have to lose?" he added softly.

He had a point there. But what if I couldn't do it? Right now, I hadn't tried, so that tiny smidgen of hope was still there, no matter how much I tried to control it.

I took a deep breath, trying to hold back the cough that wanted to come out again. He was right. I needed to at least try. I would be no worse off than I was now if it didn't work. And maybe much better.

"What if I look stupid?"

That startled him. "What?"

"If I can change, what will my transformed self even look like?" I asked. "What if I look ridiculous or monstrous?"

"I can't believe this," he said, exasperated. "Who the fuck cares if you look stupid? At least you'll be healed! Of all the..."

He started muttering to himself but I thought it was a valid concern. Not one that would stop me from at least trying. But valid.

"How am I going to get out of bed?" I asked, trying to be practical now that I'd come around to the only real choice.

"You don't have to. Hold on."

There was a tug in my arm as he pulled the IV out, but I hardly even noticed it over everything else that hurt. They must have given me something pretty damn strong for the pain, which I truly appreciated.

"I'm going to wheel the bed to the elevator," Ashur explained.

Suddenly the world around me was in disorienting motion that I couldn't see. Even the subtle vibration of the hospital bed wheels caused pain to nearly take my breath away. I held it to spare my ribs further torture as he pushed.

Ow ow ow. I gritted my teeth as it seemed the trip would never end. Thank God for drugs.

I must have lost some time because when I was with it again, I could feel the blazing warmth of the radiated sun.

"We're on the roof, it's safe for you to change here," Ashur informed me.

"Okay. Wait—what if I do change? Won't I crush the bed?"

"I don't give a fuck about the bed," he growled.

All right then. Sheesh.

I had to grit my teeth as a fresh wave of pain tried to take me down. This was not fun at all. When I could breathe again, I asked him what he wanted me to do.

"Close your eyes."

That much I could do. I closed my eyes.

"Now, I want you to picture a dragon—"

"But I'm also part phoenix," I interrupted. "What if I don't turn into a dragon?"

"I can smell the dragon in you," he explained. "At least as strong as the phoenix. I don't know what your actual genetic makeup is, but as you said, you're an odd mix. Who knows what will come out on top? Mia, go with what I can sense. The dragon is there, just under the surface. You need to focus on it."

I didn't know about that. But I was willing to try.

"Imagine every part of that dragon," he continued in a quiet voice. "The scales. The teeth. The claws. The wings. It doesn't have to look exactly like you will look—it's more the idea of a dragon that you need to envision."

Okay. I'd never done anything like this. It was kind of like meditation, which I wasn't great at but I tried my best. I focused as hard as I could, picturing the parts as he listed them off. I lay still for excruciatingly long minutes, trying to block everything out, picturing every tiny detail that came to mind.

Nothing.

Apart from the beginnings of a headache to add to all my other problems. My heart started sinking.

"Nothing's happening," I said, letting out a painful huff of frustration as I pointed out the obvious.

What if I really couldn't change? How long would it take me to recover? How much would I recover really? I knew how badly burn victims could be damaged. I could lose a lot of normal functions. While I wasn't a vain person, the thought of being forever scarred from this-- I blocked out that thought. It wasn't productive or helpful.

"Keep trying," Ashur said patiently. "You can't expect it to just happen. This is your first time. It's like anything else— you need practice." I grabbed onto the confidence in his voice, using it to bolster my own. "Now, picture it again. The light shining off your scales, the breadth of your wings..."

As he spoke, I tried something different. He kept telling me to picture myself. But I had no idea how I would look. However, I knew exactly how he looked in his dragon form.

So I pictured him.

It was simple. The image of him in his dragon form was truly seared into my mind. I remembered how he looked when I first met him. How he looked during the battle. The strength and power of him, the sheer size...

My body started to tingle.

"Focus, Mia," Ashur urged, banked excitement in his voice. "You have it!"

I remembered the grace with which he flew. And the tingles intensified.

My eyes snapped open as my body convulsed on the bed, a rush of sensation sweeping through me in an overwhelming flood. It was agony and ecstasy, going on forever and for only a moment.

The bed broke under me and my clothes ripped away as I burst out of my body.

My vision returned and sharpened until I could see clearer than I ever had before.

And the pain-- that grinding pain, hovering around me even through the haze of drugs-- it was gone. Nothing had ever, or would ever be, as radiant as the absence of pain.

I shuddered as I tried to lift my hand to my face.

A claw-tipped wing poked me on the cheek instead.

I blinked at it. Well. Shit.

CHAPTER FIFTEEN

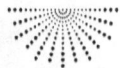

*W*here was Ashur? I glanced around and realized I was much higher up than I had been.

Oh.

I looked down. There he was. He had backed up quite a bit to give me room, and he was staring, his mouth hanging open.

"What?" I asked. Or at least, I tried to. It came out as an odd growling rather than distinguishable words.

Luckily, Ashur had experience with dragon speak. He understood what I was trying to say easily enough.

"Wow," he said, a smile starting to spread across his face. "I've never seen such a...fancy dragon."

Fancy? That was not a word I was expecting. He must have seen my confusion because he walked over next to me and jerked his chin behind me.

"Look."

I turned in the direction he'd pointed. There was a large metal storage shed in one area of the roof, tucked out of the way behind the door that led up. It was as shiny and reflective as a mirror.

I stared. Huh. And stared some more. This really wasn't what I'd been expecting to see.

A large, lavender dragon stared back at me.

Purple.

I was purple.

Did that mean I was related to those dragons that had attacked? Would the others see me and immediately attack before asking any questions? I wouldn't blame them considering what had just happened.

But there was something else I wasn't expecting at all. The reason why Ashur had described me as fancy.

My wings-- they were edged in feathers. Red feathers that fluttered when I spread my wings out.

"Those are phoenix feathers," Ashur explained from next to me. "I've never seen anything like it. But then again, I've never met anyone quite like you either."

I stared, turning this way and that.

"Whoa," Ashur laughed, stepping back as I almost hit him with my tail. The very end of it was also adorned with a fan of feathers. "You're a lot larger now—you're going to have to learn to adjust to your size."

I craned my neck—what an odd sensation! I could bend my neck in any direction like a swan or a snake. I wanted to look at my scales from close up. They were lavender, yes, but from this close, I could see they were actually iridescent, reflecting the rays of the sun in a rainbow.

Oooh. Pretty.

I straightened quickly and had to spread my wings to steady myself. An incoming breeze caught them and I hopped back with the force of it.

And had another sudden realization. Could I fly?

I looked over at Ashur, spreading my wings out and flapping them a little. I was sure my face looked hopeful if a dragon's face could convey emotion like that.

Ashur laughed, his face suffused with humor and joy. "You want to fly?"

I nodded, probably looking ridiculous. But I just couldn't bring myself to care.

This was amazing!

I was pain-free and I was a dragon!

Or a dragon phoenix.

A dragix? Maybe a phoegon? Hmm. Maybe I could spend some time coming up with names later.

"Hold on," he said, turning and getting some distance between us. "I'm going to change so I can take the lead and catch you if there are any problems. But I want to give you some instructions first. Are you listening?"

I gave him a look. No, I was just going to jump off a skyscraper and hope for the best.

He grinned. "Glad to see you're feeling better," he said, his face turning serious for a moment. "I couldn't imagine..." he trailed off. I really wanted to know what he was going to say, but he shrugged it off. "All right, we're pretty high up, which should work in our favor. I'll jump off first and spread my wings to glide. You jump off a few seconds after me. We should be able to ride the currents for a while—you'll get the hang of steering pretty quickly. It's instinctive once you're in the air. If we're getting too low, I'll use my wings to rise. You just have to follow my lead. Got it?"

I nodded again, watching him.

"All right, good."

He closed his eyes and burst into his dragon shape between one breath and the next, his clothes shredding away, so much faster than me that it was like he'd been fast forwarded.

Maybe it just took practice. Maybe I'd be that fast after a decade.

Now that he'd changed, I could see that he was much bigger than I was. Maybe half again my size. He looked back over his impressive shoulder as he walked to the edge of the rooftop that had no railing. I could actually appreciate that feature now.

I took a step towards him. Satisfied that I would follow, he turned. And with no further ado, launched himself off the edge.

Oh man.

I moved forward gingerly, looking down. He rode the current back up, circling around and using his wings to hover only yards away from me, but to the side so he wasn't in the way.

Waiting and watching.

I looked down. That was a long way down, even if I had sprouted wings.

Okay, I needed to not look down.

Piece of cake.

I forced my head up while Ashur watched patiently. I couldn't show that I was afraid. He'd never let me live it down. From personal experience involving doing things I didn't want to do, I knew it would only get more difficult the longer I waited. I needed to just do it.

Moving back a little, I inhaled. And inhaled some more. Wow, I could really take in a lot of air with these lungs!

Okay, focus. I needed to stop delaying. I had this. No problem. I was a strong, powerful woman. Er, dragon.

One. Two.

Three!

My heart was pounding as I launched myself off the building and snapped my wings open like I'd seen Ashur do.

If my eyes were shut, nobody had to know that apart from Ashur. Who hopefully didn't notice.

My stomach rose as I dropped, but then the wind caught me. My body strained with the force of it, but I was rising, my wings adjusting automatically to ride the current.

Was I doing it? I wasn't in free fall anymore. I carefully opened one eye to check. And then the other.

The city spread out below me.

I was doing it! I was flying! Did this mean I never had to be afraid of heights again?

Ashur shot passed my side in a blur of gold until he was in front of me, his large body graceful and gorgeous. In his element. He belonged in the sky.

I was shaky and ungainly next to him, but I was still in the air. I called that a win. I wasn't nearly as good at maneuvering as he was, but he adjusted, making sure I could keep up with him as he led me past the city, spread out like a miniature model below us.

My heart was beating so fast in my chest as a joy like I'd never experienced before suffused me. I could fly!

I grinned as I followed Ashur across the length of the city, which was much larger than I'd realized. It took time to fly across all of it. And then we were over the flat, bleached desert. It looked different from this high up. Like the distance made it somehow smaller.

Ashur flapped his wings lazily and I followed suit, my body knowing what to do without conscious thought. Like I was born to fly.

We glided through the hot air with the sun beating down on us, farther than I'd ever dreamed I would go. We flew over other city domes, spaced so far apart I knew I'd never have seen them otherwise.

We flew for hours. And I loved every minute of it. It was

like a piece of my life that was missing clicked into place. A piece I didn't even know I needed.

I adjusted as Ashur changed course. Why had we veered in this direction? Then something caught my eye in the distance. Squinting, I focused, my eyes so sharp I could make out details even from miles away.

The ground beneath us had started rising and falling, the flatness giving away to hills and valleys. The crack in the earth that I was so focused on slowly coalesced into a deep valley as we drew near.

And then there was something that shouldn't have been there. Color. Vibrant green color.

Was that...?

My eyes widened as I started making out individual trees, clearings, the sparkling clarity of a river of water. A river that led to a large, glittering lake.

Ashur lazily descended towards it and I automatically followed, my eyes glued to the sight in front of me.

But-- trees were gone. Natural ones anyway. And these looked natural. Vegetation was gone but for what we carefully cultivated ourselves. Even as I thought that, I couldn't stop staring.

The scents hit me as we came even closer. The scent of water, of green things.

Of *life*.

Ashur aimed for the strip of clearing around the lake, extending his wings as he neared the ground. I watched carefully as he used his wings as a kind of parachute, cupping the air to slow his descent, cushioning his fall. He changed as soon as his feet hit the ground and turned to look at me.

"Run when your feet hit the ground! You'll need to get rid of the momentum! It takes time to learn how to land in a smaller area!" he shouted up at me.

All right then. I swallowed as I aimed for the grass next to him. Run when I hit. Got it.

I cupped my wings, trying to slow as the ground rushed up at me. It didn't work quite as well as I'd hoped. I was still going fast. Too fast. I grunted as my feet hit the slight cushion of the green grass, running for all I was worth. Well, waddling. I wasn't really built to run well in this form.

No, it didn't go well. And yes, I probably looked like an idiot. It didn't help that I tripped and face planted, skidding to a stop with my nose buried in the rich earth.

Perfect.

The sound of footsteps ran towards me even as Ashur's laughter grew louder.

"Are you all right?" he asked, still chuckling as he bent down to look into my eye on one side.

I glared at him.

He just grinned back. "I promise not to tell anyone," he offered. "For a price."

I huffed out a breath. Figured.

"Picture your human self," he said encouragingly. "You'll find the change easier now that you've done it once. It's exactly the same only in the other direction. And you know how your human self looks."

He was right that I knew how I looked as a human. And I never expected to form a sentence like that. I closed my eyes and pictured myself. Any minute now... I'm sure it was coming... And...

Nothing.

I needed to put more oomph into it somehow. Ashur must have thought the same.

"Think of your dark hair, the pale gold of your skin," Ashur murmured. "That ridiculous rack. That round butt."

My eyes snapped open and I glared at him.

He raised his hands and backed away with a smirk, his eyes laughing. "Just trying to help."

I shut my eyes again and focused on my face. On my amber eyes. The small scar above my lip from when I'd had my head bashed against a wall. Not one of my best moments. The arch of my eyebrows.

The tingling meant it was working. I kept focusing on the details as the change started to ramp up, the tingles intensifying. Ashur was right. It was faster this time.

My body...collapsed, for lack of a better word. Folding in on itself. It was weirdly disconcerting, more so than growing larger because it was like parts of me were just disappearing. I wondered where all that mass went.

And then the tingling faded away.

When I opened my eyes again, I could still see, and I was looking up at Ashur from a sprawled position on my stomach. He crouched down in front of me, his eyes scanning my naked back. I was about to make a smart comment, but his eyes met mine solemnly. There was only relief in them.

"You're healed," he murmured, reaching out to smooth his large, warm hand down my back. "Perfect."

My breath caught in my throat at that touch and his eyes met mine again, his hand stilling on my back. Those crystal blue eyes darkened as he realized his touch was affecting me.

I cleared my throat and sat up because I was too vulnerable lying down on the ground. Mistake. Ashur's eyes dropped right down to my breasts, his jaw clenched.

"Fuck," he muttered, abruptly standing and turning away, giving me an unimpeded view of his muscled back and the hard curve of his ass. "Sorry."

I swallowed, my heart beating faster as I stared at him. At the expanse of gleaming skin stretched over his hard body. He was physical perfection. The wide shoulders, his muscled back, the deep furrow of his spine, the definition in his arms and legs that was apparent even when he was relaxed, like now. The little indents at the small of his back that I wanted to kiss. He was just as large and impressive in this form as his other one.

My hands itched to touch him.

I stilled at that thought.

Why the hell not? I was more alive than ever. And maybe a little reckless—I'd just flown through the air for miles on my own wings. I slowly got to my feet and took a step forward. I just wanted to feel good for a bit. To stop worrying about everything else and live for the moment. Maybe I wasn't being completely logical, but I didn't care.

I watched my hand as I placed it on his smooth back.

He sucked in a breath.

"Careful," he warned, his voice deep, a little rough. It sent a shiver down my spine. "Is this really what you want?"

I swallowed, sliding my hand around his body. Taking hold of the thick erection I'd only caught a glimpse of.

That was answer enough for him.

Growling, he slid out of my hold and turned around. His eyes were narrowed as he cupped my ass and drew me up his body. And then his mouth was on mine.

That initial contact electrified every inch of me.

Hard and deep, the kiss was all-encompassing from the word go. And it was just what I wanted. I groaned, lifting my legs to wrap them around his slim waist, his erection throbbing against my already-wet folds at the shift in position.

I rubbed myself against him, wanting him too much to be self-conscious.

He groaned, taking us down to the ground. The bed of grass was soft under my back. He left my mouth and kissed his way down my neck to my breasts, his hands sliding impatiently over my skin.

Cupping my breasts. Sliding over the curve of my waist.

Squeezing my hips. His mouth closed over a hardened nipple as his fingers found me and slid in easily. I was already so wet for him.

I cried out, arching up into him as my hands slid into the rough silk of his hair, my eyes on the bright blue of the sky above us.

He bit down on my other nipple and soothed the sting with his tongue before kissing his way right down my stomach, his breath hot on my skin. Going where I wanted him most. He gripped my thighs, pushed them apart, and buried his face against me.

I moaned, my hands clenching in his hair as his tongue found me, licked me, worked me hard. Expertly.

I came embarrassingly fast, writhing under his mouth. I tried to stay silent, but I couldn't keep whimpers from escaping.

But he didn't stop as I began to come down. Taking my clit into his mouth, he started sucking and flicking his tongue against me as he slid another finger into me.

I cried out, trying to move away, but he held me down easily as he forced me to ride out the next orgasm. And then another one. Until my body went completely limp and I just lay there, trying to catch my breath.

Saturated with pleasure.

He gave me one last kiss, letting out a low laugh as I twitched in response. He moved back up my body and took me into his arms, holding me close.

I frowned, opening my eyes to stare at his flushed face. His erection was hard and pulsing against my stomach.

"Don't you want...?"

I slid my hand down, but he caught it before I could touch him.

"No," he growled, flipping me over so he could spoon me from behind and I couldn't touch him where I really wanted to. "You've been through a lot. And I don't take advantage of women."

"What if I want to be taken advantage of?" I asked archly, irritated at his high-handedness.

"Then I'll be happy to oblige. Later," he replied implacably, his hand closing over my breast.

I rolled my eyes. "You're not *my* Dragon Lord," I muttered.

His chest shook behind me in a silent laugh.

"I bet I could get you to change your mind," he purred, sliding his thick thigh between mine. "Just not right now."

I sighed. But didn't push it more than that. Maybe he was right. Maybe I'd regret this later. But man. I'm damn sure it would have been worth it.

Fine. This wasn't going any further. But then I really needed to get my mind off that erection digging into my butt.

"How does this place exist?" I asked, my eyes going to the lush trees. It was a testament to how thoroughly he could distract me that I hadn't asked the question earlier. This place was a literal miracle. The air composition, the lack of unpolluted water, and the searing sun weren't friendly to anything green. Hardy cacti were the only exception. Or that's what we were taught anyway. "I thought they couldn't survive out here. And how is there a lake?"

He hummed behind me.

"If there's one thing that's for certain, it's that nature will always find a way to survive," he finally said. "We believe the water comes from underground, though why it's decided to bubble up now is a mystery. Our own botanists think there was some kind of mutation that allowed these trees to grow here like this, creating an environment for the smaller grasses and other flora. And this isn't the only place like this, though they are few and far between. Rare enough so that they're all considered neutral zones for phoenixes and dragons."

"What about humans?" I asked.

"They never come out this far," he replied. "Most of these places aren't anywhere near city domes and are surrounded by dragon or phoenix territories." He shrugged. "And we figure it's a fair trade. Humans don't let us into the domes and we don't tell them about these places."

I wanted to argue, but I thought about everyone who'd want to immediately strip this place bare. I was impressed the dragons and phoenixes had been able to preserve the places even without humans knowing. Maybe it was better that more people didn't know.

"We protect it from each other too," he added. "Nobody can take anything or leave anything. Not unless they want to face down all of us."

"Hmm." That would be quite a deterrent.

We let silence descend after that, enjoying the life around us. It was so...peaceful. I was experiencing a lot of things that I'd never experienced before in a ridiculously short amount of time. Not all of it had been good. But this...this was worth everything else. And I wanted to enjoy it as much as I could.

With that thought in mind, I lay still, wrapped in Ashur's arms, for a long time. Soaking in the lush greenery. Enjoying the sound of running water and his hot body against mine.

It was perfection.

An oasis in the madness that had become my life. But, like everything, it couldn't last forever. We both had to go back to the real world.

I needed to get back to Omari.

Ashur kissed the back of my neck and I knew it was time. When we finally stood up again, I looked over at Ashur.

"I don't know if I can change again," I admitted. I was

exhausted in an indefinable way. Like I'd overused a muscle I didn't even know I had.

"The change will take it out of you the first few times, until you get used to it," he explained, sliding my hair behind my ear, his expression soft. He was relaxed out here. It softened some of his edges, made me want to hug him close. "I'll change and you can ride back on me."

Wait. What?

"Um..." I looked at him dubiously.

He smiled. "Don't worry. I won't let you fall."

I wasn't so sure about that but I didn't have another choice. He changed and ducked down so I could climb onto his back. I'd never climbed anything butt naked, most definitely not a dragon.

It was...interesting. His scales actually gave me a pretty good grip, so that was something. Lying down on his upper back, I wrapped my arms around his neck and gripped him with my thighs.

"This would be a lot easier if you came with a seat belt," I muttered as I got comfortable.

He let out an odd sound that must have been a dragon laugh.

"Okay, I'm ready," I announced, closing my eyes.

He didn't wait for another indication. He spread his wings and took off. I was still sorta freaked about the height but his hide was smooth, and there was enough friction that my grip was secure.

So long as I didn't open my eyes, I was fine.

When I first laid eyes on Ashur, I never would have thought I'd be riding him naked.

Well.

Not like this anyway.

CHAPTER SIXTEEN

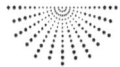

When we got back to Ashur's building, Enzi was waiting on the roof. His face was slack with shock as he watched us land. Guess he didn't see a naked woman riding the Dragon Lord every day. My mind immediately went to the gutter again. Was there no way to describe this without it sounding dirty?

And how was I supposed to get off Ashur while I was in my birthday suit and Enzi was staring? When I didn't slide off Ashur's back, he turned his head to look at me questioningly.

"Uh. Can I get something to wear?"

Ashur looked over at Enzi.

"Oh. Oh, yes!" he stammered, turning away and hurrying over to a small chest near the door. He opened it up and came back with a t-shirt and some sweatpants. I caught them when he threw them at me. He politely turned around before I could ask. Scooting off Ashur, I dressed quickly. Ashur changed back to his human form, completely at ease with his nudity. I wondered if I'd ever get to that point.

"You can turn around," Ashur called out after I was dressed.

Enzi turned, his cheeks a little pink tinged. He probably had exactly the right idea about what had been going on between Ashur and me. My cheeks were just as pink.

"The security team wanted to go over possible changes with you," he explained, very pointedly not looking at me. "When I couldn't find you, I was informed you'd flown away with an unknown dragon who'd adorned herself with feathers. Since you didn't alert anyone, I put two and two together and came up here to wait for you." He paused. "I didn't realize you'd be gone so long."

Adorned? "I didn't have a hot glue gun and feathers at the ready to 'adorn' myself."

Enzi smirked at that. "That was just what I heard."

Ashur nodded. "Thank you, Enzi. Tell them I'll be right there."

Enzi took his cue to leave.

An expectant silence descended. Oh boy. Did we have to have a talk now? I really hated talks. Talking about emotions might have been above heights on my list of things I didn't like.

"You better go take care of that," I said lamely, hoping to avoid the talk.

Ashur chuckled, walking closer and wrapping an arm around my waist. "You can't just ignore what happened between us."

The fact that he was still naked was really distracting. "Probably you should put some clothes on."

He flashed me a grin. And then gave me a hard kiss that left me dazed, leaning me back and pressing his thick thigh between my legs. He knew exactly what he was doing. Sneaky bastard. Stepping back after my heart rate was up, he gave me a sloppy salute.

"Something to think about. I'll talk to you later, Mia Hill."

And then he was gone. Kind of like Batman from those really old movies. I wondered if he'd show up if I shone a dragon spotlight in the sky. And, yes, I was definitely avoiding the issue.

Shaking my head at myself, I went inside and down to my room to shower and change. I needed to find Omari. Fully dressed and feeling more myself, I left the room.

It was a little odd not to have either Hathai or Enzi with me, watching my every move. And, for once, I wanted someone to point me in the right direction. Figured. I decided that going down to the lobby would at least ensure I could ask about Omari's whereabouts, so jogged over to the elevator.

When I stepped inside and the doors closed, I got a good look at myself. Wow. I drew closer to the shiny doors. I looked . . . really good. Like I'd had the world's best night's sleep or indulged in a week's worth of spa treatments or something. Huh. It must have been related to the change.

I was still puzzling over that when the doors opened to reveal the lobby. Wait. Was that food? I immediately turned towards the smell, my feet carrying me that way on autopilot. Only then did I realize exactly how hungry I was.

I followed the sounds of glassware and cutlery down a hall to the side. A pair of double doors were wide open at the end. As I got closer, I realized the doors led to what amounted to a mess hall. Dozens of people were sitting at the family-style tables, food laid out in the center of each.

As I walked in, a slight hush fell over the room as people turned to stare.

Okaaay.

Did I have something on my face? Or could they tell what I'd been up to? That would be really embarrassing.

"Mia!"

I turned at the familiar voice, smiling as Omari ran over to me, a giant smile on his face. I crouched down to catch him in a hug, something in me finally relaxing at finding out he was all right. He pulled back after a moment, his face indignant.

"They wouldn't let me see you! They said you were sick and couldn't see anyone!" He paused for a breath and stared at me. "You don't look like you're sick," he accused.

I laughed. He was right.

"I *was* sick," I said, holding his hands. "But I'm much better now. Have you been doing okay without me? Playing with your friends?"

His face lit up at mention of his friends. "Yes! Cara and I went outside with Hathai and we helped pick up some of the rocks from the fight!"

It took me a second to figure out that he probably meant the rubble from the buildings.

"Ah. It was nice of you to help. What else did you do?"

"Oh, we went on the swings and..."

I let his happy chatter fill me as I stood up. I looked around, meeting eyes as people stared. I wasn't really one to let that kind of thing go. If they had something to say, they could come out and say it. But they didn't. Everyone slowly went back to their conversations. I'd have to figure out what that was about later.

Omari led me over to where he'd been eating with the other kids, and I sat down next to him, answering when he had a question, but otherwise just listening. I took an empty plate and filled it up, digging in as I kept up my side of the conversation. He finally got everything he wanted to say out and sat there. Seeing an opening, I pointed at his plate.

"Eat."

I didn't have to tell him twice. He loved to eat. Kid after my own heart. As I stuffed myself, my thoughts went back to why I was here in the first place. To take Omari to his family in the phoenix territory.

At least, I was assuming it was his family who'd hired me.

But now, with everything that happened... I didn't know if that was the best course of action anymore. There was a lot to consider. As I sat next to Omari while he happily chatted about his new friends, I thought about what would have happened had I died. Or even not recovered from those severe burns.

Yes, Ashur kept telling me taking Omari to the phoenix territory wasn't a good idea. But would Omari have had a place here? As welcoming as everyone was being right now, what would happen when he got older? If he was able to change into a phoenix?

Prejudice didn't just go away. Especially not the kind steeped in history and deliberately stoked throughout the years.

If he didn't have a place here or in the human city domes, where would he have gone? Who would have taken him in and cared for him? If he had family who cared enough about him to hire me to bring him to them, I needed to follow through for Omari's sake.

The idea of not always having the chatterbox next to me sent a pang through my heart. I needed to remember he wasn't mine to keep.

By the time we finished the meal, it was time to head up for bed. Ashur and I had spent the whole day away and I couldn't regret it. Even if it stirred up emotions that weren't helpful at all. The Dragon Lord wasn't mine to keep either.

Shaking my head at myself, I tuned back in to the present.

"Come on, Omari," I said, standing up from the table. "Time for bed."

He didn't argue with me, waving goodbye to some people and sliding his hand into mine. We got on the elevator alone.

Now was as good a time to tell him as any. We'd been here too long at this point anyway.

"We're leaving to go to the phoenix territory tomorrow morning," I told Omari, glancing down at him.

"Tomorrow?" he asked, biting his lip. "Can't we stay a little longer?"

This was what I was afraid of. I shook my head, crouching down so I could look him in the eye.

"I'm sure you'll make new friends," I reassured him, smiling. "And there will be people there who care about you."

He shook his head and stepped close to wrap his arms around my neck.

"I want to stay with you," he whispered. "Can I?"

My heart almost broke as I wrapped my arms around him, closing my eyes. I swallowed past the knot in my throat. I really wanted to say yes but that wasn't the responsible thing to do. And I owed it to Omari to be responsible.

"How about this," I offered. "We go. I wait, to make sure you feel comfortable there. And if you don't, I take you back with me. How does that sound?"

"You won't leave me if I want to stay with you instead?" he asked hopefully, pulling back so he could see my face. "You promise?"

"I promise," I said solemnly. And really hoped I could keep it.

"Okay."

He still didn't sound happy about it, but I'd take the acceptance. When the elevator doors opened again, we were both quiet as we walked down the hall to our room. Neither of us were thrilled with this decision, but I had to be strong. It was the right thing to do.

When we turned the corner, I was distracted from my musings. Someone was waiting for us.

Ashur straightened from where he'd been leaning against the wall in front of our door.

"Hi Ashur!" Omari chirped, happy to see him. "Mia says it's time for bed."

Ashur smiled. "Looks like it is," he said, squeezing Omari's shoulder.

"Omari, why don't you go in and brush your teeth?" I said, opening the door to the room. "I'll be right there."

He looked between me and Ashur. "Okay," he said, walking inside without argument.

Sometimes I got the disconcerting impression Omari understood more than I thought another child would. I closed the door most of the way and turned to Ashur.

I needed to tell him too. Needed to know if he was still keeping us prisoner.

"We're leaving for the phoenix territory in the morning," I said, meeting his eyes. "Omari might have people there who care about him. I can't justify not following through and finding out if that's the case."

Ashur's jaw clenched and he looked away. He took a moment to speak. "You shouldn't go," he said in a quiet voice. "It isn't safe." He turned back to me, his expression imploring. "I don't trust whoever hired you."

Well, him and me both.

"I have to go see," I said just as quietly, not wanting Omari to overhear. "Be sure I'm making the best decision for Omari."

He sighed, shaking his head. "You're making a mistake. And not a small one."

"It's mine to make."

He nodded, taking a step closer. I tilted my head back to keep the eye contact as his hand came up to cup the side of my face.

"That it is," he said, his eyes dropping to my lips. "But I'm not done with you, Mia."

Before I could respond, his mouth came down on mine in a soft, gentle, lingering kiss. My eyes were half closed by the time he pulled back. He walked away. I touched my lips as he disappeared down the hall. They tingled from that light touch.

The Dragon Lord packed a punch.

But it didn't change my decision to leave. It couldn't. Sighing, I went into our room and closed the door.

Couldn't anything be simple?

CHAPTER SEVENTEEN

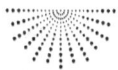

*a*s I got ready the next morning, I tried to shake off the glum mood that wanted to take hold of me. We needed to leave. Omari needed to be taken to his people.

I knew that.

My life was even more messed up than it had been just a week ago. No matter what Omari wanted or how much I cared about him, going to the phoenix territory was the right thing to do.

It didn't help that when I wasn't worrying about Omari, I was thinking about Ashur. Which was just as futile, really. I couldn't stay here either. My life was back in the city dome. And it wasn't as if we had any kind of commitment to each other. We'd fooled around once. That did not a relationship make. And Ashur might want me now, but I couldn't stay on the off chance it might become something more.

"Ready?" I asked Omari as I stood up with my bag.

The bow I'd used during the attack was beyond repair from the blast of fire I'd taken, so I'd had to throw it away. Luckily I had the backup in the car.

"Yes," Omari said, still a little glum.

"Come on," I said, smiling as I took his hand. "It'll be fine. Everybody loves you here—I'm sure everyone will love you there too."

He nodded. But he didn't look any more convinced than I was. Still, we both wore our brave faces. When we walked out into the hall, there still wasn't a guard there. I guess they'd given up on watching us.

We walked down the hall and to the elevator. This was the last time I'd do that. It made me sad, though I wasn't usually so sentimental. I needed to focus. This wasn't a vacation. I was on a job. It would be best if I kept that in mind.

I wasn't some naive schoolgirl with stars in my eyes either.

We made it down to the first floor, and Omari immediately spotted his group of tiny friends.

"Can I go say bye?" he asked wistfully, his eyes on the group.

How I could I say no to that? He was running over before the "yes" had completely left my mouth.

"They're going to miss him too." I looked up to see Enzi and Hathai walking up to me.

Hathai nodded in greeting. "All the kids love Omari," she confirmed, her face more impassive than Enzi's. She took in the bag slung over my shoulder and my holstered weapons. "Leaving?"

I nodded.

"I need to get Omari back to his people. Are you here to stop me?" I'd have to come up with a different way out if they were. But both of them shook their heads, a strange smile on Enzi's face. "No. Just wanted to wish you luck on your journey." Hmm. I narrowed my eyes at him. Something was off.

"Thanks," I said cautiously.

Omari ran back to me. "Bye Hathai! Bye Enzi!"

Both of their faces softened and they returned his enthusiastic hugs.

"Come on, Omari," I called, walking towards the open doors. "Time to hit the road."

Nobody else stopped us as we walked out onto the street and turned towards the parking garage. I firmly squashed my disappointment that Ashur hadn't at least come to say goodbye. It was for the best. I might have made a fool of myself if he had.

"How long will it take to get there?" Omari asked as we entered the dimmer garage area.

"Well..."

I trailed off and came to a stop as I discovered what was waiting for us by the car. Or, rather, who was waiting.

"Ashur!" Omari exclaimed, jumping up and down in excitement. "Are you coming with us?"

Ashur smiled, straightening from where he'd been leaning on the car. "Yes." He looked at me. "Someone has to watch out for you guys out there."

I stared at him.

"Omari, get in the car," I ordered, unlocking the door.

"But—"

"Now."

"Okay," he said, letting out a put upon sigh as he climbed in. "I never get to hear anything good." He closed the door with a little more force than necessary.

As soon as he was safely out of earshot, I turned to Ashur again. "What are you doing?" I hissed, trying to keep my voice down. "You can't come with us!"

"Sure I can," he said in an infuriatingly calm voice. "I can't let you two go out there alone—who knows what you could run into? Look at what happened when you ventured out here—we caught you immediately."

True. But it still burned, damn it.

"You'll just make it harder for us," I tried. "The phoenixes won't be happy to see me bringing a dragon with me. Especially a Dragon Lord!"

"I won't cross over the boundary," he reasoned. "No reason for them to be angry if I don't trespass."

"What about your people? Don't you need to be here to run things?"

"I have a close-knit group of trusted people who can handle anything that could happen while I'm gone." He took a step closer, his eyes scanning my face. "You don't have to like it or even agree," he murmured. "Hell, you can even pretend I'm not there at all since I'm planning on flying above you so I can keep watch."

I was at a loss. I didn't know what to say. This was more than I expected. More than I wanted to expect. I didn't want to start depending on him. That was the road to disappointment. And I already had enough of that in my life.

"Ashur-- " I started.

"I'm not letting you go alone," he said firmly, his eyes flinty now. "Deal with it."

With one last look at me, he turned and strode out of the garage. Probably to climb onto a roof and change.

I stood, watching him leave. He was always walking away from me. What did this mean? Did he feel obligated? Did he feel like we were now his responsibility? Or was there more to it? Did he actually care?

"Mia?"

I turned to see Omari sticking his head out the open door.

"Are we leaving?"

I sighed. It didn't matter why. I couldn't control Ashur. Whether he came or didn't, we needed to leave.

"Yes. We're leaving."

I got into the car. It was odd, like I hadn't driven it in

months though it had only been days. So much had happened since we first sat inside. Shaking off the disconcerting feeling, I maneuvered the car out of the garage. I'd taken a look at the map this morning, so I already knew where I needed to go.

As we drove out onto the street, the people drifted to the sides to let us through, watching our progress. The farther we drove from the center of the bustling city, the fewer people we came across. Then the buildings abruptly turned from beautiful and glimmering to old and dilapidated. Shells of old cars lined the sides of the streets, stacked on top of sidewalks like the dragons had come through and picked them up from the middle to make the road usable. Broken windows peered out at us, the rooms inside dark even during the daytime.

And it was quiet. Eerily so.

The hairs on the back of my neck prickled as we drove through the ruins of our past. Maybe it wasn't completely empty. I didn't really believe in ghosts. But isn't this where they would be if they existed?

"Does anyone live here?" Omari asked in a quiet voice, his eyes scanning the windows just like mine were.

"No," I said, catching movement out of the corner of my eye. But nothing was there when I turned to look. Unsettling to say the least. I really wouldn't want to be driving out here alone at night.

As we took another turn and I judged we were nearing the city's edge, a giant shadow flew over us. A giant dragon-shaped shadow.

"Ashur!" Omari exclaimed, looking up with a big grin on his face.

I immediately felt a little safer.

Damn it.

CHAPTER EIGHTEEN

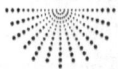

The desert spread out in front of us, the sun beating down on the dry earth. Ashur glided lazily above us, high enough now that the sound of him cutting through the air couldn't be heard. So far, the journey had been pretty uneventful, which I was thankful for. I'd had enough excitement to last me a lifetime.

We'd stopped to rest, with Ashur coming down and eating with us, sleeping in the back of the car. When morning came, we started out at the first light of dawn. As we kept driving, the flatness of the land slowly started to change, with large rock formations appearing. I would have gone around them, but it would add more time and distance to the journey unnecessarily. According to the map, the distance across wouldn't take too long if I drove straight through.

Still, I made sure to angle away from the city dome that I knew was to the east. I didn't particularly want to run into anybody. I didn't trust anyone inside a city dome and I definitely wouldn't trust anyone leaving one.

The rock formations grew until parts had actual overhangs over the path I had to drive under. Though, honestly, I didn't even know if it could be called a path. Path implied it was used pretty regularly. The ground continued to slowly dip until the rocks rose up on either side of the car. They were beautiful, their deep orange striations glowing in the light.

I glanced over at Omari, who was playing with a hand-held vid game one of the kids must have given him. At least he wasn't bored.

The area in front of us dipped down once again, steeper this time, until the rock walls on either side were at least three stories tall. The overhang extended far enough that I couldn't see the sky directly above us. It was almost a tunnel. I turned on the lights as the area in front grew dimmer. Hopefully there was a way out of there or I was going to have to double back and try to find another route through.

The headlights hit a pile of rubble directly in our path.

"Shit," I muttered. And immediately looked over at Omari guiltily.

He finally looked up from his tiny screen at the abrupt stop. "Where are we?" he asked, looking around.

I started reversing. "We hit a dead end," I explained as we slowly passed by the smaller connecting tunnels and paths. "I'm just going to head back and try to find a different way out."

I came to an abrupt stop once again. There was a large rock behind us, blocking the way we'd just come. I knew it wasn't there just a minute ago when I came in. My stomach sank. Turning in my seat, I grabbed my sword, my knives already at my hips.

"What's wrong?" Omari asked, his eyes frightened as he watched me.

Shapes started to emerge from the shadows, from the various crevices in the rocks.

I'd driven right into an ambush.

Who or why, I didn't know. But there was no innocent reason to set up something like this.

I looked up, but I already knew there was no way Ashur could see what was going on. Not unless he had x-ray vision. The rocky overhangs completely hid us from aerial view.

And I would need Ashur's strength to move that rock.

If I was by myself, I'd make a run for it on foot. There was still space to shimmy by the side of the rock. If I ran fast enough, I might have been able to get to a clear area and flag Ashur down.

But I wasn't alone.

"Stay in the car, Omari," I said grimly as I counted at least eight people.

"But—"

"In the car," I ordered, opening the door and stepping out. Chances of getting out of this unscathed were slim.

I closed the door behind myself.

"What do you want?" I called out, gripping the sword's hilt in my hand.

A spare man in his fourth decade, hair shaved down to mask a receding hairline, stepped forward. His shirt was open down to the middle of his torso, showcasing his concave chest. He looked to the side and revealed a tattoo of a chain link covering the right side of his neck.

Slave traders.

Shit. If they just wanted to steal things, I might have been able to bargain with them. But they didn't want things. They wanted people.

I braced my feet, watching the others slowly inching closer.

"Hello, sweetheart," the first man cat-called, spreading his arms wide. "What brings you out here?"

He grinned and that was apparently their cue to attack.

I didn't waste time. I speared the first man who lunged at me. This was a life or death situation and Omari was counting on me not being the one to die. I considered shifting, but I knew there was no way the slavers would let me stand still long enough to concentrate.

I braced my foot against the man's chest and pulled the sword out, hacking out at another man, this one burly with a goatee and no shirt. He might have looked ridiculous, but he knew how to fight. He blocked me easily with his own sword and started pushing down, smiling at me. I pulled back.

A contest of strength would get me nowhere.

Shrugging, I stepped back and threw the sword at him.

He was not expecting that at all. He jumped back and I used the distraction to throw one of my smaller knives at him, the hilt sprouting from the side of his neck. He went down as a stocky woman came in with her fists.

I knew I wasn't going to win, but desperation gave me strength and stamina I wouldn't have otherwise had. I dodged her attack and managed to land a good shot to her stomach. And another to the side of her face.

I was fighting against a fate that really was worse than death.

"Mia!"

My blood chilled in my veins and the woman caught me with a right hook, though I blocked enough of the blow that it took away the brunt of the power. I took two quick steps back and looked over to see the man who had spoken cradling Omari against the front of his body.

Holding the tip of a short dagger near his vulnerable throat.

"Let him go," I growled, taking a step towards him.

"Stop right there," he ordered as he brought the knife closer to Omari's neck.

I froze, my chest tight.

"Drop your knives."

There was no choice. I dropped them.

"Hold your hands out in front of you, wrists together."

Another man, this one with an eye that was sewn shut, came over with rope and quickly tied me up. He'd obviously had plenty of practice.

"Good," the leader said with satisfaction. "Now, we're going to the city dome with the two of you. And I'm going to keep the little guy here with me the entire way." He smiled, his eyes cold. "You aren't going to try to pull anything, are you now?"

I shook my head, picturing slamming my knee into his face. But he had Omari. I couldn't do anything while it would risk him.

"Excellent." He turned to his people. "Get rid of those bodies and let's move out." He looked at the car, his eyes calculating. "We'll come back later for that."

The guy who'd tied me up pushed me forward, making me stumble. Catching my balance, I walked forward, through one of the crevices that led to an open space not that far away. It was still under an overhang, in the shadows. I didn't know which way things would go if they realized neither Omari nor I were fully human.

They had a couple of enclosed vehicles and I was led to one while Omari was led to the other.

"Mia?" Omari asked, seeing that we were being separated.

"I need to keep him with me," I tried.

"He'll make do on his own," the ringleader said.

I swallowed, really wanting to strangle the guy. "It's okay, Omari," I said, knowing that wasn't much reassurance. "I'll see you in the city dome, okay?"

He nodded, shrinking into himself. These guys were really going to regret this. I'd make sure of it. But for now, I cooperated and watched.

"Get in the car." Another shove. Excellent manners. I slid into the car, between two men who really needed showers.

"She'll fetch a good price, huh?" the driver commented. He had a short beard and a build that had once been athletic before he'd packed on the pounds, though he still looked strong. "Even has all her teeth!"

The other men laughed.

"Yes, but who knows how long that will last," the stocky woman snapped, glaring back at me from the front.

"Don't touch the merchandise, Ellie," the one-eyed man next to me warned. "You know the boss will make you regret it. Cuts into our profits too much."

"Shut up, Ernie," she muttered, turning to the front again.

They kept bickering back and forth while I tried to hold my breath and not take in the stink of unwashed bodies. At one point I shut my eyes and pictured my dragon self, but the jerky drive, my roiling stomach and the occasional jab of an elbow meant I never felt the familiar tingle.

The drive wasn't actually that long, and most of it was in and out of the rock formations, with good cover. I didn't know if Ashur would be able to track us. I had to figure out how to escape on my own.

When we reached the city dome, I wondered how we were going to get in past the guards, which showed I still had some naivety left after all. The clean-cut guard looked in the car and glanced at my tied hands.

I wondered if this was the time to kick up a fuss. Maybe the guard could actually help me. Then I realized the driver was transferring money to the guard's account. He raised his watch and tapped at it.

"Pleasure doing business with you, gentlemen," he said with a wide smile. "Go on in."

There went that idea.

We went through the familiar two-chamber system and

entered the dome. I felt claustrophobic for the first time ever. I'd gotten too used to the open sky. And if possible, the streets we inched through were even narrower than the ones I was used to. Or maybe I'd just gotten too accustomed to the dragon way of life with the wide streets and generally spacious areas.

I watched as they drove us deeper into the city, but I knew I wouldn't be able to keep things straight, not when we wove in and out of cramped streets, twisting and turning too many times to count.

The farther we went, the worse the surroundings got, which I guess wasn't all that surprising. When we finally stopped and got out, the reek of trash greeted me. Liquor and drug stores lined the streets. Working women strutted around, swaying their hips to properly display their wares. Most looked as high as the latest street drug could make them.

The other car, the one with Omari, was nowhere in sight.

"Where's Omari?" I demanded as I was pushed forward once again, this time to a staircase that hugged the side of a gray building in a narrow alley.

"Not here," Ellie replied shortly. "Best you worry about yourself now, bitch."

All right. Step one—slam Ellie's head against a hard surface, preferably multiple times.

Step two—escape.

Step three—find Omari.

Step four—get out of the city dome and make our way back to the car and Ashur.

I climbed up the steps as I made my list. What I found when we walked through the door at the top was the stuff of nightmares. The stench of unwashed bodies, alcohol, and decay was almost overwhelming.

I was led into a small network of apartments that had

probably started off their lives separated. Now, I couldn't even make out the exterior doors that must have been sealed shut. I glanced around at the barred windows and the women wandering around in various states of undress. Some were lying on dirty mattresses, passed out. Sleeping, drunk, or high, I didn't know.

Others were awake, their eyes watching me, though with a dullness that told me they'd never get out even if by some miracle they physically escaped. This place would forever live inside them.

I looked away as I passed a room full of women on their backs, men, who'd no doubt paid for the opportunity, on top of them.

Bile rose from my stomach and burned my throat.

Some of these women had likely chosen to be here, drawn by money, drugs, or both. But most had been forced into this. I was finally led to a tiny room that had must have been a closet at some point. It had room for a mattress inside. That was it.

"In here." I was pushed inside. Couldn't they just tell me where they wanted me to go? The door closed and locked behind me. The only light was from the tiny barred window, maybe a foot wide, at the other end of the miniscule room.

Yup.

I was screwed.

CHAPTER NINETEEN

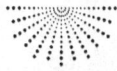

I leaned against the wall. The lighting wasn't great in there, but I knew I didn't want to touch that bare, dingy mattress. They still hadn't taken the rope off my wrists, so I started there. It wasn't as tight as it could have been. I'd made sure to keep my wrists slightly apart when he'd wrapped them.

After twisting, turning, and more than a few curse words, I was able to shove the coil off my wrists, sacrificing a little skin in the process. I stowed the rope in my pocket. Might be able to use it later.

I stepped over the thin mattress to look out at the street below. I was guessing the few skimpily dressed and heavily made-up women out there were part of this operation as well. I couldn't see these guys allowing anyone else on what they considered their turf.

Okay.

My plan was simple. When the door opened next, I needed to be ready to break free. I was certain most of those women out there didn't start out like that. They were probably going to try to inject me with whatever drug they used to keep everyone in line, to addict them until they became a slave to the drug and were really stuck here.

Until they'd do anything for another hit.

I couldn't wait around for that to happen to me. I had to get out as quickly as I could.

I stood against the wall, behind the door. I took the rope back out of my pocket, wrapped it around each of my hands, and tested its strength.

It would do.

Then I stood still, waiting for the door to open.

It didn't take long before someone decided to come check up on me. The door creaked open and the big guy with the beard stepped inside, his hands already undoing his pants.

More nervous bile. This crap was going to give me ulcers.

"Time to break you in..." he started, but then trailed off as he noticed the room was seemingly empty.

He took another step in to look. How convenient.

I stepped up behind him and threw the loop over his head, tightening the rope against his throat and pulling him back with it. He was strong, but he hadn't expected an attack like this one and he wasn't trained for it. His hands grabbed at the rope, clawing at his throat when he would have been better off trying to get at me.

He panicked. Poor baby.

I pulled on the rope with all of my strength, my arms straining as he tried to get traction with his feet and failed. It took some time for him to stop struggling. I didn't let up even then, not until I was sure he wasn't going to get up.

Breathing hard from the effort, I pulled the rope off his throat, looking away from the raw gash that had opened up his skin. He chose this life. I refused to feel badly. The world was better off without him.

Pressing my lips together, I quickly searched him. They'd taken my weapons but Beard here had decided to keep one of my knives. Liberating it from him, along with a retractable baton, I stepped out of the room and closed the door behind me. Nobody was directly outside the door, giving me a chance to gather myself.

Moving quietly, I retraced the steps we'd taken through the maze of melded apartments. I passed women who stared at me suspiciously, but no other guards.

Sloppy. I appreciated the lack of effort.

Then I reached the room that had an actual exterior door. Ellie was standing in front of it, her eyes on the three girls at work to one side. She didn't look up until I was almost on her.

Her eyes widened as I swung the baton at her head. She ducked down quickly. But I was ready with my knee. The crunch when I made contact with her face was really satisfying.

She cried out, but her hands didn't go to her face. She wasn't quite as idiotic as her friend. She swept my feet out from under me, sending me to the floor.

That was my fault.

Then she was on top of me, her broken nose dripping blood and her face twisted in rage. I guess she didn't like to be on the other end of the abuse. Too fucking bad, bitch.

Grunting, I managed to get my feet between us as she tried to wrap her hands around my throat. And then I heaved, causing her to fly across the room. It would be satisfying to finish this, but I'd thrown her far enough that it had left the door clear, and I didn't know when or if anybody else would show.

I needed to run, not waste more time. No matter how gratifying it would be. I yanked the door open and almost flew down the stairs as Ellie's shouts followed me down.

Reaching the street, my eye fell on the nearest alley and I bolted straight for it. I needed to get as much distance between me and that hellhole as I could. I was so focused on that, I didn't realize the alley wasn't empty. A tall figure stepped into my path and I ran right into him.

I tried to step back, but strong hands closed over my elbows. Oh no he didn't. I slammed my foot down on his instep and twisted free of his hold as he cursed. No way was I letting someone manhandle me again. I skirted around him, ready to keep running.

"Mia!"

Huh? I stopped, whirling around. The man pushed his hood down.

"Ashur?"

"Yes, Ashur," he said in a strained voice. "That's the welcome I get for sneaking my way in here to rescue you?"

I blinked at him.

"I think I just rescued myself," I pointed out. "And how did you get in here?"

"You really think dragons and phoenixes stay out of these places?" he asked with a smirk.

I shook my head. That really didn't matter right now.

"We need to move," I said, grabbing his hand and pulling him forward as I continued down the alley. "They might be coming after me."

"How did you get out?" he asked, keeping up easily.

"I asked nicely."

He chuckled as we came out into a different street and moved in front of me. "Hold on, I know somewhere we can lie low until night," he said, turning us in the other direction.

"I need to find Omari," I argued, letting him pull me along.

"I know where he is," he said over his shoulder as we turned onto a nice residential street. "But we have a better chance of getting him out safely after dark when there won't be as many people there."

"You know where he is?"

"Yes," he murmured, squeezing my hand as we walked with the crowd. "I tracked him first but it looked like a no go. I didn't want to barge in and possibly get him hurt." He stopped in front of a short flight of stairs that led down from the street to a door. "Here we are."

I glanced around at the street. We hadn't been walking that long, but this place was a complete one-eighty from where I'd just been. One of the oddities of city domes. I followed him down the stairs, watching as he unlocked the door with a code and a retinal scan.

"This is your place?" I asked curiously as I followed him inside.

"Yes, I bought it for the skein," he explained as I walked in behind him. "In case someone found themselves here and needed a place to stay. I keyed everyone in."

He turned on the lights and I looked around at the sleek, modern kitchen and living area, a hall leading to what must be bedrooms in the back.

"It's nice," I commented. It was really jarring coming here after where I'd just been. Also, now that I was in a relatively safe space, I realized exactly how much I needed a shower. I almost needed it more for my mental health.

"Can I use the shower?" I asked.

"Sure. First door on the right—everything you need should be in there. There are spare clothes in the cabinet under the sink."

That was one thing about dragons—they always had spare clothes conveniently stashed nearby. I went down the hall to the bathroom, which was just as sleek and modern as the rest of the place, built efficiently small. It had the same palette of grays, browns, and creams that managed to look welcoming as well as very contemporary. I easily found spare toothbrushes and toiletries and brushed my teeth first before shucking my clothes and jumping in the shower.

Ah. Amazing, glorious water.

A good scrub later, I dried off and found the ubiquitous sweats and t-shirts under the sink. They were starting to become pretty familiar. I wasn't complaining though—I was just happy I had clean clothes to change into. I gave my hair a quick brush and left it to air dry as I padded back out to the kitchen.

Ashur had used the time to take a shower himself. His hair was as wet as mine and he'd only bothered putting on sweatpants, leaving his top half bare.

I took in the muscled lines of his body, the smooth skin. How did he manage to always be so effortlessly sexy? I turned away as he poured a glass of water. Now was not the time to stare.

Still keyed up, I started pacing, looking at the paintings on the walls, touching one of the tables. I turned to see him watching me, leaning against the kitchen counter.

"Are you sure we have to wait until nightfall?" I asked, pushing my hair back. "I don't want Omari there any longer than necessary."

He nodded. "I understand. I don't either. But this is the safest way to do it."

I sighed. "Okay." I tried to sit down on the surprisingly comfortable couch. But then had to stand again, too worried and anxious to sit still.

"Come here," Ashur finally said, pulling me into his arms when I turned to pace past him again. "You need to rest and relax while you can. You're going to wear yourself out like this."

I leaned against his warm body and shook my head. "I can't."

"You can." His hands slid down to cup my butt. "And I know just the thing to help," he said, his voice husky.

I leaned back to look at his face. To say what, I don't know. But he took the opportunity to set his mouth against mine. At the contact, I simply broke. All the anger, frustration, fear, it all poured out of me in that kiss.

And he took it all, groaning as he lifted me and turned to set me on the counter, stepping between my legs, his mouth not leaving mine.

I needed this.

I needed him.

"Ashur," I gasped, breaking the kiss, my hands in his hair.

"I have you, Mia," he whispered, kissing my ear, the side of my neck, nuzzling the side of my face. "I have you."

And then his mouth was back on mine. And I let myself let everything go for a little while.

CHAPTER TWENTY

I lost myself in the kiss, in his taste. In how he wasn't afraid to show exactly how much he wanted me.

He shaped my breasts through my shirt, but then let out a frustrated sound and grabbed the bottom edge. I raised my arms and he tugged it over my head. Groaning, he cupped and squeezed my now-naked curves, but only briefly before he tucked his fingers into the waistband of my sweats and pulled them down too. I was completely naked in under ten seconds.

He didn't waste time joining me. He pushed his own sweats down, his thick erection bobbing as he stepped close to me again, his hands sliding up my thighs slowly as he stared at me, as if savoring the sight.

I slid my hands down his hard chest and his ripped abdomen, enjoying the leashed power of him. This time nothing would keep me from wrapping my hand around the thick length of his erection. He stilled, watching, his breath catching.

I stroked up and down a few times. I could touch the silky

hardness of him forever. Reaching the tip, I rubbed my thumb over it, spreading the wetness there. He groaned and took hold of my wrist to stop me.

I looked up, wondering why.

"That's enough," he said, his voice a little ragged. "I don't want to go in your hand."

Then his own hands were on my hips and he was pulling me forward, to the very edge of the counter. Leaving me spread open and at the perfect height.

He didn't delay any more.

In one slow thrust, he sank in all the way, squeezing inexorably past my tightness. I gasped as he moaned, the suddenness of the invasion making my entire body arch. When he was seated with his hips pressed against mine, I was completely filled and surrounded by him. He started thrusting.

Crying out, I wrapped my arms around his neck, tucking my face against him as his body moved inside me, against me. The counter was cool and slick under my butt, his body hot against my front, his muscles working in beautiful harmony.

It was hard, hot, fast. It was exactly what I needed in that moment. I cried out as my orgasm surprised me, my nails digging into Ashur's back as I thrust against him, grinding against him, wanting more. He rode me through it, drawing it out, pushing me hard.

When I finally relaxed onto the counter, he was still hard and throbbing inside me. He picked me up.

"Bed," he muttered, turning and walking us down the hall to the bedroom. It was just as modern and nice as the rest of the place. All I cared about was that the bed was nice and soft underneath me when he lowered us onto it.

I sighed as he layered his body over me, his mouth coming down on mine as he started thrusting again, still buried deep inside me. This time the rhythm was slow and deep, and just as perfect.

I smoothed my hands down his back and cupped the hard curve of his ass, squeezing as he kept up the thrusts, even and slow.

Breaking the kiss, he rose up on his arms, his eyes meeting mine. He was inside me, but somehow the eye contact was more intimate than the physical joining of our bodies. Maybe because he was seeing me with all my shields down.

"Mia," he sighed, burying his face against the side of my neck. His hand reached between us, sliding down my stomach, right to where we were connected. His fingers found my clit, rubbing, softly pinching.

And that was it.

The orgasm was slow and deep this time rather than an explosion, the waves of sensation sliding through my body in a delicious river.

"Ashur," I gasped, my fingernails digging into his back as my legs tightened around his hips. But when I'd come down, Ashur was still just as hard inside me.

I groaned. He must have been trying to kill me. Though what a way to go.

"One more," he muttered before flipping me over onto my front and sliding back into me, the angle a little more shallow this time. He slid his arm under me, his fingers finding my clit again. And then he started thrusting, the movement sliding me against his fingertips just right.

"Oh," I gasped, sliding one knee up and gripping the edge of the mattress.

He kissed the back of my neck, his breathing harsh, his body sliding against mine easily, both of us sweating by this point.

"You come this time," I ordered, my voice strained as another orgasm built.

"That...won't be...a problem," he said, his voice gritty, his thrusts increasing in speed and strength. The rhythm turned erratic as he neared his own end. A few more thrusts. And then he slammed in as deep as he could go, and his cock jerked inside me. His body stiffened on top of mine as he came silently, his hot breath washing over my neck.

The warmth of his orgasm inside me triggered my own. I pushed back against him, trying to catch my breath as his hand squeezed down on my hip, his entire body shuddering as the orgasm rushed through him. We strained against each other, the connection intense.

It was more than just our bodies coming together.

Finally, he pulled out with a sigh, his hand smoothing down my back. He dropped down next to me, wrapping his arms around me and pulling me in against him. I lay there with my head pillowed against his chest, his steady heartbeat soothing.

Until reality started tapping against my mind.

"This wasn't the best idea," I murmured, even as I snuggled in closer. So sue me. I was weak.

"It was the best idea," he countered, sliding his hand down to cup my butt. "Excellent. Superb even."

I shook my head, exasperated. "My life is in the city dome," I pointed out.

"It doesn't have to be."

"Yes, it does. That's where my business is. And I'm not the stay-at-home-in-an-apron type."

He chuckled. "I didn't say you were. And you're way over-thinking this."

"Maybe you're under-thinking it," I muttered.

He was quiet for a bit, like he was formulating how to put his thoughts into words.

"Sometimes, things are only as complicated as you decide to make them," he said quietly. "But we'll talk about it later, when we have more time. For now, we can just agree to disagree."

I sighed. He was right. I didn't want to waste this time talking about an unrealistic future. So I closed my eyes and just enjoyed the moment and hoped I wouldn't regret letting myself fall deeper into whatever this was with Ashur.

CHAPTER TWENTY-ONE

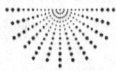

*W*e lay there until the sun went down, our arms and legs tangled together, touching everywhere. But it was more about comfort. We had gotten up to throw our clothes in the wash, so we pulled them out of the dryer and dressed.

I was jittery, ready to go get Omari back. Hoping nothing had happened to him while we'd had to wait. It was like stepping back into reality as we closed the door to the apartment behind us. And it was a harsh one.

"This way," Ashur directed, turning and jogging down the street.

I followed at the easy pace he set.

The building we went to was a few blocks away, not that far from where I had been held. They probably wanted to keep their human merchandise conveniently close. My jaw tightened at that thought. The slave trade was technically illegal, but everyone knew it existed. There were just too many people willing to take a payout to look the other way. The people who were captured were usually like me—from different city domes. So nobody would report us missing in the place we actually ended up.

The block where they were keeping Omari was a little better than the one they'd taken me to, but not by much. There were a few more-normal stores littered among the liquor and pawnshops. And I didn't see as many obvious drug deals going on. I guess that was a pretty low bar to pass.

Ashur took us to a shadowy doorway down the street, where we could see the place but were hidden enough not to be noticed. He scanned the street once we were out of sight.

"Okay, good," he muttered, his eyes on the entrance to the tall, narrow building that had seen better days. Boarded-up windows on the first floor and peeling paint seemed to be the norm here. "There are only two guards here now. I don't know what floor they took Omari to, but I'm guessing they control the whole building or the guards wouldn't be near the entrance door."

That made sense.

"So...have a plan?" I asked hopefully.

He shook his head. "Bash their heads in and grab Omari?"

I nodded. "Looks like we're going to have to just wing it," I commented, my eyes on the two men smoking and chatting to each other.

"Good thing I can sprout two," Ashur said in a low voice.

I rolled my eyes and he grinned. Shaking my head, I turned my attention back to the guards. I didn't recognize them, which was a plus. Hopefully they wouldn't recognize me either. They didn't look like the sharpest sentries either. They glanced as people walked by, but they were more distracted than they should have been by their conversation. Still, they would definitely notice us walking up to them.

"Four between the two of us."

"Just stop," I said, smiling despite myself.

We watched for a bit longer to lower the chances of being

surprised by something. The street wasn't filled with people here, but neither was it deserted.

"They aren't expecting us," I said after a few minutes. "Just step into the crowd and split them?"

Ashur nodded, his smile sharp. Predatory. I wouldn't want to be on the receiving end of that smile.

"Works for me," he said.

We crossed the street and fell into step behind a trio, two men and a woman. We stayed close enough so that it looked like we might be with them.

"I'll take Beanie," Ashur said when we were only a few yards away, referring to the larger of the two, a tight cap squeezed onto his head. It had the unfortunate effect of making his disproportionately small head look even smaller. That meant I had the thinner guy with the bloodshot eyes.

"Got it."

The two men were still smoking as we came level with them, their eyes passing over us without recognition, though they both lingered on Ashur. When you were that big, it was difficult to blend or look in any way nonthreatening. Though with Ashur, it was more than his height or his muscle that made him look like a threat.

He was a predator through and through and it showed.

So I went first.

"Hey," I said with a smile, walking up to the skinny guy as Ashur continued to move forward, drawing even with the other one. They both turned their attention to me. The thin one started to smile, his eyes scanning me.

"Hey there—"

My fist to his mouth interrupted what I was sure was going to be a riveting come-on.

I extended the baton with a flick to the side and followed the punch up with a hard hit to his temple, the crunch of bone unmistakable. He went down hard. He wasn't coming up any time soon, if ever. I didn't waste even a little regret on him. Not when I knew what they were up to here.

Ashur had the other man already on the ground. He was in even worse shape than my guy. Ashur nodded at me and we moved forward in tandem to the door leading in.

But the metal door was locked, both with a keypad and a print scanner. This would take some time to get open. Time that we didn't have.

"How are we—"

"Don't worry, I just need a second," Ashur reassured me, putting a hand on the doorknob.

What was he doing?

I watched as the metal under his hand slowly turned red and then started melting. I knew intellectually that dragons were excellent metalworkers. The undisputed best, really. But knowing it and seeing why were two very different things. Less than a minute later, there was a hole in the door and Ashur was sliding it open.

"Piece of cake," he said with a wink. "I'm great at barbecues."

"I bet," I said faintly, staring at the still-glowing door. That was impressive. And more than a little scary. I shook it off. I'd have plenty of time to pepper him with questions later. We didn't have a lot of time right now. If whoever was in charge didn't notice the guards were down, the state of the door would give us away, if security cameras hadn't already caught us.

The door opened into a narrow hall that extended towards the back of the building with a set of steep stairs to the left. Ashur moved forward down the hall but then hesitated and turned back.

"What is it?" I asked in a low voice.

"I think I could scent Omari here," he said, moving back to the door. "But not farther down the hall."

We started climbing up the concrete steps, Ashur taking in deeper breaths, frowning as he tried to tease the scents apart. We stopped on the first floor and Ashur opened the door leading from the flight of stairs. But then he stopped, shook his head, and turned back. We kept going like that, with Ashur checking and then coming back.

It wasn't a lightning-fast method, but it was definitely much faster than having to physically check each room. The fact that there weren't any guards on those floors was also a dead giveaway

He caught Omari's scent again on the fifth floor.

Unfortunately, as soon as he opened the battered door, a guard turned around to look at us. It was the man with one eye. His good eye fell on me and recognition washed over his face.

"You—" he started, taking a step forward as he pulled his large, dirty knife. I didn't want to know what was caked on it.

Ashur stepped in front of me and grabbed the guy by the wrist, pulling him forward and swinging him around to slam against the wall.

I drew my knife to slit his throat. Fast and clean. It was better than he deserved, though I didn't enjoy doing it. He slid down, his hands grabbing at his throat as he bled out.

We turned away and kept going. At the end, the hall formed a T-intersection. Ashur hesitated. But then I thought I heard a sound.

"Left, I think," I said.

He nodded, and we jogged down that way to another door. This one opened up into what could only be called a prison. One entire side of the hall was lined with cells, the metal bars leaving no doubt as to what the intention was here.

Ashur's face was grim as we walked inside. The first cell

held a little girl, maybe seven. She was curled up on the bed. The next one held a boy, close to twelve. He glared out at us sullenly.

And it continued.

One after the other.

All ten cells were occupied with boys and girls of various ages.

We walked down the entire length, my eyes searching for Omari. But still nothing. My hope was starting to wane as we approached the last one. What if they took him somewhere else? What if they--

"Mia!"

My heart skipped a beat as Omari rushed over to the bars.

"Hey," I replied, trying to speak around the knot in my throat as I ran to his cell, reaching through the bars to take his hands. "Are you okay? Did they hurt you?"

"I'm okay," he said, his hands tight on mine, his eyes big. "But can we leave now?"

I choked on a laugh. "Yes, we can leave now."

"Step back so I can open this up," Ashur ordered.

"Step back, Omari," I repeated. "We'll have you out in a second."

He let go of my hands reluctantly and took a few steps back, watching Ashur with interested eyes. Ashur lifted his hand, and the heat from it was much more noticeable now in closed quarters. He melted the old-school lock right off. It didn't stand a chance.

Omari shot out as soon as the door slid open. I grabbed him and picked him up, relief making my knees weak as I held him close. He was alive and in one piece. The tightly wound part inside of me finally relaxed. But we didn't have time to waste here.

"What about the rest of them?" I asked Ashur, looking down the line of cells.

Most of the kids had gotten up to look out at us. Some of them had the wariness that came with being on the street too long. Others still had some hope in their eyes.

Ashur nodded. "Step back," he ordered the boy in the cell next to ours.

He complied immediately. We didn't have a lot of time, but we couldn't just leave them there. It took maybe an extra ten minutes to get them all out.

"What do we do with them?" I wondered, staring at the nine kids.

Ashur grabbed the three oldest.

"Take everyone to this address," he said, showing them his watch. "Here." He took it off and gave it to the girl who was on the verge of becoming a woman, her pretty face holding the promise of beauty that was probably the reason she was here in the first place. "Can you get there?"

She nodded, looking over at the boy who had stared at us when we'd walked in.

He nodded too. "What do we do when we're there?" he asked, his eyes too old for his face.

"Give me the watch." The girl handed it back to Ashur. "A lady I know will come to that same address and help you, okay?"

"All right," the girl said, her intelligent eyes direct, but still wary.

"Good. Follow us out. There isn't much time."

Ashur made a call as we strode out. The woman on the other end took the directions and agreed to meet the children without asking questions. The older kids paired up with the younger ones and followed us down, back to the first floor. Out on the street, I hesitated with Omari's hand in mine.

"Shouldn't we go with them?" I asked, worried about sending them out alone.

"They'll attract less attention without us. And those are kids who know the streets. They'll be fine."

"But..."

I knew firsthand what kind of trouble kids could get into out there alone. I turned to look for them. They'd already disappeared. I hoped they made it safely.

"Come on," Ashur said, taking my free hand. "There's a garage around the corner where I keep a car. We'll take it out."

We didn't bother trying to blend in this time. We ran, trying to get as far as we could as fast as we could. When Omari got tired, Ashur swept him onto his back and we kept going. We finally turned into a garage that was in a much better part of town and got into an equally high-end car. It looked shiny and new.

"Just how much money do you have?" I asked suspiciously as I helped Omari buckle up in the back.

"Enough," Ashur replied as I slid in to the front seat. "Why? Trying to figure out if it would be worth it to be with me?" He turned to look at me as he slid out onto the street.

I snorted. "I'm not worried about the size of your wallet."

He smiled as he faced forward, merging smoothly into traffic. "You shouldn't be." He paused. "It's huge. Just like the rest of me." He winked.

"You're insufferable," I said, shaking my head.

"I'm rich, handsome, and I really like you." He glanced over at me as we reached the line leading out of the dome. "You should really be more open to this."

"And so humble too," I muttered.

"Does Ashur want to be your boyfriend?" Omari piped up from the back.

"No," I said firmly.

"Yes," Ashur said at the same time, looking back at Omari. "Maybe you can convince her I'm not so bad."

"That's low," I said, shaking my head.

"I fight to win," he replied, completely unrepentant.

"I don't know if you should be Mia's boyfriend," Omari said thoughtfully. "You have a lot going on in your life. You wouldn't have enough time for her."

I let out a surprised laugh as Ashur shook his head wryly.

"Blocked by a six-year-old," he muttered.

"Serves you right."

We reached the security booth leading out of the dome and the guard stepped out. He bent down to take a look at me and then Omari.

"I'm sorry, sir, but you aren't authorized to leave," he said.

"I've already deposited the money," Ashur said calmly.

Of course he bribed the guards. That was exactly what the slave traders did. The guard swallowed and looked away.

"The traders here could make life really hard for me," he said, his upper lip already sweating.

Ah. They knew we'd escaped and were willing to pay to keep us.

"So could I," Ashur said quietly. "And who says they have to know you let us out?"

The guard hesitated.

"Get rid of today's footage. I'll double the amount."

That had him nodding and stepping back. I didn't know if it was the money or the path to cover his ass, and at that point I didn't care. I let out a relieved sigh as we pulled forward into the first chamber.

"Those slave traders need to be taken care of," Ashur said in a low voice. "The police force here is a joke."

There was no way to argue against that. The only way I could see to do it would be to take them out. That was only a short-term solution. Another group would just spring up in their place.

I breathed a sigh of relief as we drove back out into

the desert, under the cover of darkness. Things had really changed if leaving a city dome made everything safer.

"Can we go back to the car?" I asked as Ashur continued to drive with a confident ease.

"Why?" he asked. "We'll make better time if we continue straight to the phoenix territory."

"The rest of my weapons are there. And if we don't get it back now, I doubt it'll be there on the way back." I thought about it. "Assuming it's still there."

Without it, I'd have no transportation of my own.

Ashur nodded. "Car it is."

We drove back to the rock formation where we'd first been taken. I gave Ashur directions.

"Wait here," Ashur said as he parked some distance away. "I'll go make sure there aren't any nasty surprises."

"Why don't you wait here—I know exactly where to go," I argued.

Ashur glared at me. "Stay," he said firmly, stepping out of the car and striding away.

I shook my head. Men. I kept an eye out, but Ashur reappeared less than five minutes later. Nobody was lying in wait. And the car was still there.

Ashur parked his in another small, out-of-the-way section of the rock formations and got in the car with us.

"What if someone takes your car?" I said as I started up the mini tank.

Ashur shrugged. "Then they take it."

I shook my head. "Must be nice to have that much money," I commented.

Ashur nodded. "It has its uses." He was quiet for a moment. "I'd treat you like a queen, Mia," he said quietly, cognizant of the fact that Omari had fallen asleep in the back.

"I'm no queen," I countered. "And I bet the crown would chafe."

He chuckled, shaking his head. "You're a hard woman to please."

I gave him a sidelong glance. "You're welcome to stop trying." A part of me held its breath, worried he would actually stop, that he would call my bluff. Stupid.

But he didn't.

"I wasn't complaining," he murmured.

He reached out to cover my hand with his.

Oh, man.

This was getting complicated.

CHAPTER TWENTY-TWO

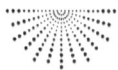

*W*e drove through the night and into the morning. Ashur took over the wheel after a few hours when he saw I was getting tired.

"You'll need to be awake for this," he said as he slid into the driver's side. "You don't know what you're going to be walking into."

How comforting. But he was right. So I closed my eyes and fell asleep almost immediately.

When I opened them again, it was to the sun shining down on us. I looked back to see Omari already chewing on one of the nutrition bars.

"Morning, Mia!"

"Hey, Omari," I said, my voice raspy. I glanced over at Ashur. "How far are we?"

"Maybe another hour," he said, looking over at me. "You should eat something and have some water. It might be time for you to take over driving while I fly."

I nodded. "Okay."

I ate quickly, the rations not horrible but not great either.

They were exactly what they were supposed to be —sustenance.

The mountains were so close now that it was like I could reach out and touch them, the craggy dips and divots more apparent as we drew closer. Like almost everywhere else, the only vegetation was hardy cacti.

This close, I could also just make out the sandstone-colored structures nestled in the mountains, dotted along a winding road. It looked picturesque. Pretty. From only a little farther away, the buildings weren't even visible. The elevated position made them pretty defensible. The phoenix city might have been pretty, but it was built with security in mind.

Ashur brought the car to a stop as I finished the bar and drank some more water. He turned to look at me, bracing his forearm on the steering wheel.

"Are you sure about this?" he asked, his face grim, his eyes worried. "It's not too late to turn around."

As I looked at his concerned face, I was tempted. Very tempted. It would be so much easier to turn around. But I had to see this through for Omari's sake.

I leaned over and kissed Ashur gently.

"I have to see," I said quietly, cupping his cheek.

He nodded. "That's what I thought," he said, turning away to look at my destination. "I'll be waiting at the edge of their territory. If I go any farther without an explicit invitation, it could mean war." He looked over at me, his frustration clear. "I can't risk it."

"I understand."

And I did. Dragging his skein into a war wouldn't make him a good or responsible leader. Which he was. Besides, he was only one individual. Any way you sliced it, if something went horribly wrong, I would rather he at least be able to leave safely than sacrifice himself in some ill-thought-out attempt to save us.

"If I don't come back out in a few hours, leave," I said.

He just gave me a look.

"Ashur," I warned.

"Mia," he parroted, opening the door and stepping out. "You can't control me."

I shook my head as I slid over to the driver's side. "There wouldn't be any point in you storming the place," I tried as he closed the door for me. "You're only one person."

He leaned in through the open window and gave me a smacking kiss. "Better come out of there as fast as you can then," he said.

And then he started stripping. Yes, I looked. How could I not? I caught the clothes he tossed to me.

"Ashur..."

"I'll see you in a few hours." He changed into his dragon shape and launched himself into the sky. That was a really unfair way to end a conversation.

Shaking my head, I started driving forward again. I glanced in the rear-view mirror to see Omari's serious face as he looked out the windshield.

"Do you want to move up front?" I asked.

He shook his head, his mood bleak. I sighed. He was just worried about a new situation. He'd be fine once he'd adjusted.

Less than an hour later, we lost Ashur's comforting shadow as we passed into phoenix territory. We were on our own.

Approximately fifteen minutes after that, three phoenixes came swooping down and landed in our path. They weren't lax with their security, which I could appreciate. I stared as I brought the car to a slow stop.

They made for a striking sight.

They weren't as large as dragons, but at maybe three-quarters the size of their counterparts, they were still more than impressive. Their feather patterns varied, from purples and reds, to oranges and yellows. One of them even had more of a green tint. And the feathers themselves glinted in the sun with a distinctly metallic sheen. Their beaks were black and glossy, as were their eyes. And their four-fingered feet were tipped with curved claws that came to razor-sharp points.

Yup.

Wouldn't want to fight that.

After I came to a stop, the predominantly orange and yellow one changed, shrinking down to a young man with a tanned skin tone that shined coppery in the sunlight. His blond hair fell around his face, reaching his shoulders, his build lean and long. His narrow face was intelligent and suspicious as he walked over to us.

I tried very hard not to look below the waist. I didn't know if I'd ever get used to casual nudity like this.

He stopped a few feet from the front of the car.

"Exit the vehicle," he ordered in a no-nonsense voice. "Now."

He might have only been in his mid-twenties at most, but he was used to being obeyed. And I had no desire to alienate anyone.

"Stay inside," I said to Omari. I said the same thing to him so much I might as well have posted a sign on the seat in front of him. He nodded, looking outside with a solemn expression.

I opened the door and stepped out, experiencing a sense of deja vu. Though I sincerely doubted this would end the way everything had with Ashur.

"Why are you trespassing?" he demanded as soon as I

was out.

I held my hands up to show I didn't have anything in them. Not that I wasn't armed. But the universal gesture of peace usually helped put people at ease.

"I was hired to deliver Omari here," I explained, nodding at the car as I watched him carefully. "I'd like to see the person in charge."

"King Emberich?" he smirked, looking back at the other two phoenixes before turning back to me. As if the idea was hilarious. That was an odd reaction.

"Yes," I confirmed, trying to understand the dynamics of what exactly was going on here.

I stood still as he walked closer. He got too close for my own comfort, but I wasn't in a position to complain. He took in a breath as he got closer and his eyes narrowed as he tilted his head to the side. Then he shook his head, not saying anything as he took a step closer to the open door.

"May I?" he asked politely, gesturing to the door. It wasn't like he was going to accept a 'no' here. I nodded.

He ducked his head inside. Then he straightened again, his face thoughtful.

"Pull forward to the beginning of the road leading up. I'll meet you there." Then he moved back and changed, the transition smooth and fast. I wondered when I'd get that good.

They flew off again and I got back in the car. "You all right?" I asked Omari as we moved forward once again.

He nodded, but he didn't say anything. Probably worried about what was going to happen now. Him and me both.

I drove forward to the where the guy was already waiting. At least he had on some clothes now so I didn't have to focus so hard on his face. Loose cotton pants and a white tunic gave him a cool, breezy look.

Now that I was at the base of the mountain, I realized there was a gondola system rigged up along the mountainside, following the road. There seemed to be several plat-forms at even points, all the way up. At the very top of the road, I could just make out a much larger building, this one complete with a dome and spires.

Someone had delusions of grandeur.

Though I guess their leader was a king. Maybe if you were a monarch some delusions were a given.

Omari and I left the car, and he took my hand imme-diately.

"It's going to be okay," I murmured as we followed our escort to the gondola. I really hoped I was right.

The gondola was luxurious. The exterior was a creamy white, while the interior was all whites and golds. There was even a carpet that was somehow still white. I didn't know what magic they used to maintain that.

We stepped inside and sat down in the bench seats lining the sides. The guy took a seat across from us, his eyes boring into me. Kind of awkward, but I could deal. We started moving up.

"What's your name?" he asked as we started passing the first section of buildings. Their light, orange-pink exteriors were topped with deeper red roofs. I could see now that parts of them were actually part of the mountain, carved out and built forward.

"Mia," I replied, turning to watch him back. "And you are?"

"Sven," he replied curtly. "Where are you from Mia?" he continued.

"A few days' ride south," I said easily, keeping it vague. "Do you know who hired us?" I figured I'd get some of my own questions in if he was asking so many.

He shook his head. "You need to talk to King Emberich about that." And then he shut his mouth and looked away. No more talking, I guess. That was fine with me.

I watched the various buildings go by instead. The paths

between them were narrow, carved into the side of the mountain. More than a few people walked them, dressed like Sven was in loose, light-colored clothes. The tops of the buildings were mostly flat, probably because there was a lot of flying from place to place.

It actually looked a lot more foreign than I expected. Whereas it seemed like the dragons were not that different from the city dome, apart from having more resources, it was like we were heading into a completely different culture here. I wondered if that translated to more than the architecture and clothing.

Sven finally broke his silence as we neared the top. "This is the palace," he announced, standing before we'd come to a complete halt. "Come."

I wondered if he spoke to everyone that way. I stepped out onto a small platform, reaching inside to pick Omari up and deposit him next to me.

There were stairs leading up to the palace. And that really was the perfect name for it. It was all domed roofs and delicate spires. The outside of it was decorated with mosaic tiles in oranges and reds, mimicking flames. Appropriate, though kind of on the nose. There were four slender towers surrounding the palace, topped with small platforms where phoenixes stood at the ready, their sharp eyes scanning the area.

When we got up to the palace's level, I realized the path to it was also a detailed mosaic, this one of a sun with the silhouette of a phoenix in front of it, the background tile blue to mimic the sky. The spires were maybe twenty stories high, the detail on them carvings rather than tile. The windows were all rectangular with rounded tops.

The double doors that formed the main entrance were thrown open, with thick columns on either side. This was more than I'd expected. I didn't know if there was any etiquette to this. I figured I would just do what I could and hope for the best. That seemed to be what I was resorting to a lot these days.

We stepped inside. I had to take a moment to look around. Ashur's place was luxurious, but it was also welcoming, open to all of his skein.

This place decidedly wasn't. It was built to intimidate, not welcome.

The ceiling was high, with intermittent glass panels letting the sunlight stream in. The floor was stone, some kind of dark and iridescent one polished to a smooth shine. I didn't know what the rest of the place was like, but we were led into what could only be termed an audience chamber. Thick columns lined either side, leading straight to a throne at the very end. A large gold monstrosity upholstered in embroidered red, set on top of a platform that needed stairs to reach it.

Overcompensating for something?

Or maybe Emberich just had horrible taste.

Other than that, the large chamber was empty of furniture, and our footsteps echoed as we walked forward. A middle-aged man sat on the throne. I took him in, curious. Tall, with silver-streaked dark hair and a short beard with a white stripe right down the center, he was dressed in clothes similar to Sven's. Similar in cut, anyway. This man's white top and loose pants were embroidered heavily in dull gold. A large ring with a ruby at its center adorned the middle finger of his right hand and a slim gold crown hugged his temples. His feet were in completely impractical golden slippers. Not that this man seemed to care much about practicality, judging by this palace.

His eyes were cool as he watched us approach, even as a small smile played over his lips. Like he was thinking of a joke only he was privy to.

"My King," Sven murmured, bowing. "Mia here says she was hired to bring Omari back to phoenix territory." His tone was remarkable for its very emptiness. Like he was trying not to betray any emotion. That told me more about Emberich than this ridiculous room.

Emberich waved him away. "Wait to the side, Sven," he ordered carelessly.

Sven bowed again and walked over to stand next to another door to the right and behind the throne, his eyes turning to me. They were as unreadable as his tone had been.

I kept Omari next to me, my hand firmly wrapped around his. His small hand trembled in mine as he stood halfway behind me, obviously scared. I wasn't expecting that. Maybe it was the build up? Omari was a pretty confident child, although I could understand his nerves. I had no idea how this was going to go either.

Maybe I should have listened to Ashur.

"Thank you for bringing my son back to me," Emberich said, his eyes on me. They flicked over to Omari, his expression not changing at all. "Good job, Omari."

What? I looked down at Omari.

"I'm sorry, Mia," he whispered, trying to tug his hand out of mine. But I held on.

The confusion must have shown on my face because Emberich chuckled.

"Who do you think hired you to come out here?" he asked. "I wanted to see my daughter. And I couldn't think of a better way to welcome you than to lead you here with your own brother."

I just stood and stared at him, hearing the words but not able to process them.

Omari was his son. That much I got. But was he saying...

"Yes," he said, as if he knew what I was thinking. "You are

my daughter, Mia. And Omari was good enough to help me get you back here, where you belong."

Wait. He'd deliberately given his son sun sickness? All in an attempt to lure me here? I licked my lips, disconnected from myself. Was this even real?

"I belong in the city dome," I finally said in a low voice.

"You belong here, with me," he countered, his voice cold, his expression hard. "Grace had no right to take you from your own father. I was inconsolable after she left with you."

Somehow, I doubted that. Mom didn't talk about my biological father much, but I'd pieced enough together to come to the conclusion that he'd most likely been abusive. And that she'd left with me to protect me from him, which meant she didn't think I'd be safe here with him.

And here I was. Caught neatly in his trap.

If he'd wanted some bonding time with me, he could have easily been on the up and up and asked for it. Instead, he'd set up this elaborate scheme to get me out here.

Manipulative, narcissistic. Maybe a sociopath.

I needed to tread lightly.

"Wouldn't it have been easier to call?" I asked lightly, my eyes scanning the area, looking for any other ways out.

I couldn't see where the door by Sven led, which meant only the door behind us was a safe bet. And that was a straight shot, with no cover if we ran.

And it would be we. No way I was leaving Omari here if he was this scared. A parent who would deliberately hurt his own child like that, put them in danger, use them...

That was no parent. Just a gene donor. This was why Omari hadn't wanted to come back.

I should have listened to him. I should have listened to Ashur.

Emberich leaned back in his throne, smiling smugly. "I

wanted you back home. With me." He gestured at me lazily. "And here you stand."

I swallowed, my stomach turning over.

This was not good.

Not good at all.

CHAPTER TWENTY-THREE

*H*ow was I going to get us out of here?

I glanced over to see Sven still watching, a slight frown on his face, as if this was news to him. And not particularly good news at that. I didn't know if Emberich had been totally open with this plan among his people, though I was guessing not from what I'd gleaned of his personality from even such a short acquaintance.

It did make more sense now why Sven had accepted my story so easily after he'd seen Omari. It wasn't my story at all that had gotten us in.

"Omari?" I asked quietly.

"Yes?" he responded in a small voice, like he was just waiting for a blow.

A blow I would never deal. He was only a child. "Do you want to stay here?"

A startled pause. I looked down at him, met his hopeful eyes.

He shook his head. "No," he said, almost in a whisper. Like he was afraid to be overheard.

All right then. That was all I needed to hear.

188

I smiled slightly as I turned back to Emberich, who was watching the exchange with interest. But not as if it really mattered what we said.

"Well, it was nice to meet you," I said as I turned to leave. "But there's been a mistake here, so we'll just be leaving..." The direct approach couldn't hurt, right?

I stopped, keeping Omari next to me as four guards appeared from behind the columns. I knew it wouldn't be this easy, but I'd been hoping I was wrong.

I turned back to Emberich.

"I'm afraid I can't let you leave," he said, his tone and expression apologetic, that smile still on his face. I really wanted to wipe it off. Maybe with a slap. Or a nice round-house. "Not before we can have some quality time together. And certainly not with my other child." He leaned forward, clearly enjoying the power he wielded here. "I'm sure you understand."

"Quality time can't be forced," I said, moving to the side so I could keep an eye on Emberich and Sven as well as the guards. "And I've been just fine without a father so far. I think I'll live."

"Have you?" he asked with raised brows. "From what I've learned, you live suppressing your phoenix side, afraid to show who you really are in that crowded cesspool of humanity you call home." He spread his hands out to his sides to draw attention to the room. "Here, you could be who you truly are, in the lap of luxury. People would kill for such a life." His smile faded. "I would advise you to take the offer or I may start to believe you aren't appropriately grateful for this opportunity."

Uh huh. I would get right on that.

"If I don't leave soon, there's going to be a whole skein of dragons showing up here."

I figured a bluff wouldn't hurt. And maybe he'd believe it

if he was aware of Ashur roaming the boundary of his territory. What I wasn't expecting was for him to throw his head back and laugh. A great big belly laugh that had him tearing up slightly as he wrapped his arms around his midsection.

"Oh, that is amusing," he said on a sigh, shaking his head as he wiped at his eyes. "Mia, Mia, Mia. If you're going to threaten someone, you need to use something that is actually intimidating." He clasped his hands, his face turning serious. "I can gather the entire phoenix population in this area at a moment's notice. We would crush one lone skein easily. Destroy them as if they never were. And while the other dragon skeins wouldn't like it, they also wouldn't fault me for it. Not when your precious Dragon Lord would be stepping into family business."

All right, he knew about Ashur. And he didn't care. I had no leverage here.

He nodded as he watched that realization dawn on my face. "Yes, that's right. Accept your fate. You will be staying here." He clapped his hands together and the rubbed them in anticipation. "Now, why don't we—"

There was a commotion just outside the door we'd come in from. We all turned to look.

"You will let me in, young man, or I will make you sorry!"

The sound of flesh hitting flesh. And then a man flying past the open doorway.

Huh.

A tall woman, maybe in her sixties, strode in. Her short cap of silky hair was mostly dark gray, her pretty face softly lined, her dark eyes vibrant and sharp. Age sat on her lightly. She wore a long, flowing dress in a pale yellow that suited her skin tone and her slender frame.

The four guards inside stepped in front of her, but King Emberich raised his hand to stop them.

"What are you doing here, Cinira?" he asked, a warning tone in his voice.

Cinira glared at the guards as she strode past them, her eyes landing on me.

"There you are," she said, shaking her head as she made her way over to us. Had I missed something? Did I know this woman? "You know exactly why I'm here, Emberich." She turned to glare at him. "I'm here to protect my grand-daughter."

I stared at her.

Again...

What?

CHAPTER TWENTY-FOUR

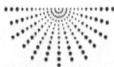

*I*f I were a fainter, I'd probably be on the floor right now. But I wasn't. Which was a good thing because then I wouldn't be able to protect myself or Omari.

So I just stood with my mouth hanging open as I stared at the woman, noting the details. There was something about the shape of her face... and her build. The way she walked. There was a resemblance, more to my mother than to me, though I could see I had her straight hair and a slight lilt to my eyes.

It wasn't definitive. But why would she lie about it? And if it was true, how could I go from no family, to a father, a grandmother, and a half-brother all in one fell swoop?

My head was spinning.

"This isn't your business, Cinira," Emberich said in a low voice. "I suggest you leave."

"It's my business more than it is yours," she snapped back and then turned to me, her voice softening. "I thought you smelled like my own when we attacked Ashur's skein. It was why I stopped Ester from killing you."

I had a flashback to the purple dragon with the distinctive

star marking that had sniffed at me. And shoved aside the dragon that had burned me before Ashur had been able to get there.

"Uh. Thanks?"

She smiled wryly at my tone.

"You look like Grace," she continued, searching my face. "You got lucky." She stared at me, though I didn't know if she found what she was looking for. "Where is she?" she asked, her face hopeful.

The familiar ache made itself known in my chest at that question. She didn't know...

"She's gone," I said quietly. "When I was twelve."

"Oh, my baby," she said, tears appearing in her eyes. "I don't know why she didn't come to me. And you, just twelve!"

She closed the distance between us and wrapped her arms around me. I wasn't much for hugging strangers. But there was something so familiar about her. And something comforting about the fact that she too knew my mother. Probably better than I did. And that she clearly grieved for her as well.

I had to struggle not to completely lose it and break down in tears.

"I have to take care of this, then we'll catch up," she whispered in my ear before pulling back. Her tone said this was a nuisance, but a manageable one. She cupped my face in her hands and smiled before stepping away and turning to Emberich.

Her back was ramrod straight as she faced him, as imperious as any queen. More impressive than Emberich. She didn't need any of the trappings.

"I'm leaving with my granddaughter," she said firmly, daring him to disagree.

"She's my daughter and she's staying," he growled.

She shook her head. "You don't want to start a conflict with me, Emberich," she warned, her face stormy. "You know I could rally enough skeins to make war between us very costly for you."

"You wouldn't reignite something so dangerous," he argued, though there was a lack of certainty in his voice.

Her smile was sharp as she caught it too. "Wouldn't I?" she asked silkily. "I believe it was you who called me—what was it? Oh, yes. A 'crazy old bitch'."

He glared at her as the guards on either side of us took a step closer.

This might have backfired...

I drew Omari behind me as I stepped closer to...my grandmother? Cinira. Cinira was easier.

But then Emberich waved his hands and the guards stood down.

"Fine," he said grudgingly, almost pouting. And then a sly glimmer appeared in his eye. "But my son stays with me."

Omari tightened his hold on me.

"I'm not leaving without Omari," I said firmly, picking him up.

Cinira nodded, as if that was a given. "We both know you don't care about that child, Emberich," she said shaking her head. "Is he worth a war where there might not be any winners?"

He glared at her. His back was stiff, his face red from anger, his hands clenched on the chair. But he relented. "You will regret crossing me today, Cinira. Make no mistake."

"I'll be waiting," she said, her smile icy. "Come, Mia." She turned and marched away from the throne, her strides long and confident.

Okay then.

The walk through that long throne room was one of the most nerve-racking minutes of my life. My whole back crawled with the urge to look around, to keep an eye on the threat. But I followed Cinira's lead and kept facing forward as we reached the flat mosaic area in front of the palace.

Sven somehow appeared in front of us as we headed to the gondola, his face carefully neutral. Looked like he always tried his best to keep his thoughts and feelings to himself. At least when he thought it counted. We were all quiet as we rode down the mountainside. It was an odd and tense few minutes.

I didn't know what Cinira was thinking, but I was afraid we'd be attacked at any moment. That Emberich was just playing games with us. He seemed like the type. But we reached the bottom of the mountain without an issue.

Sven gave us a nod and then hung back as Cinira and I walked to the car, still parked where I'd left it.

"You need to watch your back," Cinira murmured once we were out of earshot. "Emberich is known for killing his offspring. Five at last count, at least that we know of. He usually waits until they're adults so it doesn't look quite so horrifying." Her mouth tightened. "He's jealous of his power and worries they might become a threat." She looked at me as we stopped in front of the car, then glanced at Omari standing next to me.

"I'll be sure to keep that in mind." There wasn't much chance I'd forget today's encounter. But something was bugging me. "How did you know we were here?"

She smiled slightly. "Do you think everyone here is happy to have Emberich as king? Or that they agree with every-thing he does?" She shrugged. "I have informants everywhere."

That was good to know. Note to self—do not get on Cini-ra's bad side.

"Do you want a ride out of their territory?" I offered.

She smiled, this one more open and happy, though it was

still tinged with sadness. She had only just heard about her daughter's death. Though Cinira looked like she was a tough woman. I doubted she would truly let her grief out in front of me.

"That would be lovely, thank you."

So we all got in the car. In one piece. And set out across the desert.

Again.

I guess miracles did happen.

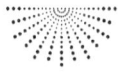

CHAPTER TWENTY-FIVE

"So you lived in that city dome your whole life?" Cinira sounded completely aghast at the thought.

"Yes," I confirmed. "It wasn't that bad. I had access to the sun when I needed it and I make a living."

"With a carrier service," she repeated.

"Yes."

She sighed.

"What?"

"Nothing," she said quickly. "It's just...so...phoenix of you."

I raised a brow and glanced over at her. "I'm technically more phoenix than dragon if I understand correctly."

She waved that away. "Your grandfather was mostly human, but he did have some dragon in him." She sighed. "I'll tell you about him some other time. Not that it matters, really," she added as we passed the phoenix boundary. I breathed a silent sigh of relief and brought the car to a stop as a familiar shadow passed overhead. I opened the door to wait.

"You'll be living with me now, of course," Cinira said as we sat there.

I turned to look at her. "Um..."

"She's not staying with you, Cinira."

I turned at Ashur's irritated voice to find him glaring at Cinira even as he leaned down to give me a kiss. His eyes turned to scan me and then Omari in the back.

"Are you okay?" he asked quietly.

"Yes, we're fine," I reassured him.

He closed his eyes and leaned his face against my neck, his big body shuddering a little. I rubbed my hand down his back, sliding my other one into his hair.

"Only because I received a message from an informant and was able to get here in time," Cinira pointed out. "So you and Omari should obviously stay with me. I can keep you safe."

Ashur raised his head and narrowed his eyes. "Be careful," he growled.

Though he didn't seem particularly surprised to see Cinira. Had he known?

"Did you know we were related?" I demanded.

His face closed off. "I wasn't sure," he hedged. When I glared at him, he relented a little. "There is a slight similarity in your scents."

"And you thought to keep this from me because...?"

"Because he likely wanted to get into your pants," Cinira remarked, obviously enjoying the discord between us.

Ashur raised a brow at that.

"Both of you can relax," I said irritably. "I'm not living with either of you. I'm going back to the city dome. You know—where my business is? Where my entire life is?"

Cinira and Ashur both broke their staring contest to look at me like I was crazy.

"Why the hell would you go back there?" Ashur finally said in an incredulous tone.

"Because I need to make a living and I have a client base

there," I explained patiently. "Now I have Omari so it's even more important that I have a steady source of income."

Ashur looked back at Omari. "Omari, don't you want to live with me?" he asked with a smile.

"Ashur, stop it," I warned. "And get in the car. I want to be farther from this place if we really need to argue about this."

That must have been a reasonable argument for him. He nodded and caught the sweatpants I threw at him. He slipped them on, got into the back seat, and I started driving again.

There was silence for a bit.

Blessed silence.

Cinira broke it.

I thought I'd have to break up another fight—I mean, she did lead an attack on Ashur's skein. Which ended up with me being badly burned. I probably had good reason to be angry, come to think of it. But I needed to hold on to that card for when it really counted.

But Cinira surprised me.

"I want to apologize," she said stiffly, turning in her seat to look at Ashur. "I thought you gold bas—" she stopped, sliding a glance at Omari who was watching her curiously. "I thought your skein was involved in my daughter's disappearance. Mia's existence obviously changes everything."

A pause.

"I understand the rationale. But you really know how to hold a grudge," Ashur finally said.

Grudgingly. But he didn't throw the apology back in her face. I'd take it.

And Cinira seemed to feel the same.

"It's one of my many talents," Cinira agreed, turning back to face the front. "Now, Mia. You should at least come see my stronghold. A visit will help you make an informed decision..."

I listened with half an ear as Cinira started listing all the positives about her stronghold.

When I glanced in the rearview mirror, it was to see Ashur talking quietly to Omari. Probably trying to convince him to harangue me into staying, no doubt. But Omari looked much more relaxed and happy now, so I let it slide.

Ashur looked up to meet my eyes. And he smiled.

My heart fluttered. It actually fluttered, like a schoolgirl in a bad teen movie. In my defense he looked even more gorgeous when he smiled. I shook my head at myself.

I was driving away from my sociopath father's palace. With my grandmother and my lover, who were apparently very old enemies. And with my half-brother who wasn't old enough yet to tie his shoes properly.

A lot had happened.

And there was a lot to still iron out.

I needed a nap.

DRAGONS & PHOENIXES (COMLETE)
Dragon Lord
Phoenix King
Shifter Queen

THE PHOENIX WARS
From the Ashes
Wings of Blood
Court of Flame

Keep reading for a preview of PHOENIX KING

SUBSCRIBE TO MIRANDA MARTIN'S MAILING LIST

Are you interested in getting the latest updates from Miranda Martin? You'll be automatically welcomed with the subscriber exclusive *Alien Prince*. Once or twice a month, Miranda sends out sneak peeks of works in progress, shiny new covers, hot deals and sales, giveaways and more

WWW.NEWSLETTER.MIRANDAMARTINROMANCE.COM

EXCLUSIVE PREVIEW: PHOENIX KING

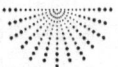

*P*rincipal Dorothy Simmons had a no-nonsense salt-and-pepper bob and glasses hooked onto those necklace chains that let you wear them like an awkwardly large accessory. Currently, she was peering down at the documents I was told I needed to bring, her mouth pursed, revealing the network of fine lines around her lips that were on their way to becoming deep lines. She must make that expression a lot.

I watched, trying not to fidget in my seat. I wasn't worried about the documents. I paid a lot for those forgeries. They were supposed to be able to withstand a thorough combing by the authorities. An elementary school principal should be a piece of cake.

She glanced up at me from above her lenses, her sharp dark eyes giving me a hard look. I tried to appear innocent.

"Hmm." She returned her attention to the paperwork.

All right. Maybe I was a little worried. I glanced behind me to make sure Omari was still doing okay in the little waiting area they had set up where kids could play. He was currently pushing a small train along a track, his round face utterly focused on the task at hand like only a six-year-old could be. For the first day of school, I'd gotten him a new, brightly colored t-shirt with some cartoon he was really excited about, new sneakers that matched, and some jeans that weren't so worn. I didn't want him to be at any more of a disadvantage than he already was.

Reassured he was fine, I turned back to Principal Simmons. With nothing else to focus on while she read, I took in her clothing. A crisp white blouse and sedate brown cardigan. I looked down at my own outfit, my beat-up synth-leather jacket, t-shirt, worn jeans, and scarred boots.

The jacket hid my knives.

Maybe I should have dressed for the part a little better.

I adjusted the package I had on my lap. I couldn't let it out of my sight until the job was done, so it had to come into the office with me. It was a plain box, but I guess carrying any kind of box wasn't exactly usual. That probably didn't help me blend much either.

She finally set the tablet down, pulled her glasses off, and folded her hands on her desk with an air of having done exactly the same far too many times to count.

"So, Mia Hill, you were just appointed Omari's guardian," she said, her eyes scanning me. She didn't seem to think I was up to the job, but it was possible that was just my own insecurity speaking. "And he's your brother?"

"Yes," I responded, trying a smile.

We only shared a father, but I didn't think that was relevant. But maybe the fact that we looked different made things even more suspicious. Omari's skin was a deeper brown than mine, his features more rounded.

Simmons didn't smile back, giving me a suspicious look instead.

Tough crowd.

I couldn't really be offended by it either. Not when she

was right to think something odd was going on. But I made sure I'd dotted all my i's and crossed all my t's. Omari needed to go to school, needed to have a life that was as normal as I could make it while running my own business, and hiding the fact that neither of us were exactly human.

"I see." She looked back at Omari. "He is going to have to be assessed, of course, but for now we can put him with his age group."

"Great," I said. "That would be great."

She nodded. "Omari," she called out firmly.

Omari looked up, a questioning expression on his face.

"Are you ready for your first day of school?" she asked with a much warmer expression than she showed me.

Omari looked over at me, clearly not knowing how to respond.

"Can I have a minute to speak with him?" I asked, already standing up to go over there.

"Yes, of course."

I crouched in front of Omari so my back was to Simmons, shielding him and giving us a smidge of privacy.

"What's wrong?" I asked directly. "I thought you were excited to go to school, to make new friends?"

He wouldn't meet my eyes, looking down at the table with the train tracks set up.

"Omari? Come on, you can tell me." I set my hand down on his shoulder, squeezing it.

He finally met my eyes, his own fearful. "What if nobody likes me? What if I'm not smart enough? Do I have to go to school? Why can't I just go to work with you?"

I sighed. I completely understood his fear. The unknown was scary.

"Everyone will like you," I said patiently, fully believing it. Omari was a sweet kid. "I know that for sure, because you're amazing. And I know you're really, really smart. You know why?"

He shook his head. "Why?"

"Because you're my brother."

That made him smile a little. "That doesn't mean I'm smart."

"Of course it does," I said confidently. "It means you're very smart. Don't you think I'm smart?"

He nodded. "Yes."

Whew. Thank God. Anything else would have been quite a blow to the ego and ended this line of reasoning right there.

"Then you are too. No way my own brother wouldn't be smart," I scoffed. "Not possible."

"But why do I have to come here?" he reiterated, apparently not satisfied with that reassurance alone.

"Because it's the law," I said firmly. "And because school teaches you things you won't learn on your own."

He still didn't look convinced. A different tactic was called for.

"Okay. Look—how about a deal?"

He straightened a little, hope infusing his face. "A deal?"

"Yes. You try going to school. If in a month you don't like it, we'll look for another one you might like better. Sound good?"

"Um." He screwed up his face. "Is that my only option?"

I chuckled. "I'm afraid so, kid. So, what do you say? Think you can brave the unknown?"

He looked down, shrugging. "I guess so."

I needed to bring out the big guns. That face was breaking my heart.

"And after school, you can have one of Jacob's brownies."

That had him sitting up, his face suddenly bright. "A big

one?" he asked hopefully, his big brown eyes looking at me imploringly. That was a hard look to say no to.

"A huge one," I promised.

"Okay. I'll try."

I resisted the urge to pump my fists in the air. Crisis averted! This one was a nail-biter. I didn't know how to be a sister, let alone a guardian. I really hoped I was doing things right.

"Hug?" I asked, stretching my arms out.

He immediately wrapped his around me, giving me a hug so tight I swear I could feel my ribs bend. He was going to be really strong really soon. I let out a silent breath of relief when he let go.

"All right." I stood up and Omari followed my lead. "Let's do this."

He nodded, his little chin thrust out in determination. "Let's do this," he parroted, marching forward next to me to Principal Simmons's desk. "I'm ready to go to school."

I could see the stern school administrator hiding her amusement. Would you look at that? Even she wasn't immune to Omari's charm.

"I can see that, young man," she said, standing up. "And I'm ready to take you to your classroom. You're going to love Ms. Nguyen."

And then we were all stepping out into the hall and trooping down to Omari's class. The narrow hall was empty, class already having begun for the day. Through the doors came the sounds of kids talking in some rooms and teachers lecturing in others.

When we stopped at the end of the hall and Principal Simmons opened the door, I peered in with Omari to take in the class. Maybe twenty or so kids were seated at tiny desks created especially for six-year-olds. The walls were decorated with colorful art projects done by little hands, and smells of glue and candy filled the air. Ms. Nguyen was at the front, a tall, thin woman with a smooth, dark ponytail, dressed in a soft yellow twinset, sensible flats on her feet. The epitome of an elementary school teacher.

She looked over as the door opened, a smile on her face.

"I have a new student for you, Ms. Nguyen..."

I watched from the doorway as Omari followed Simmons in and Ms. Nguyen introduced him to the class. I could see he was feeling shy, but he waved and went over to the desk the teacher indicated without an issue.

When he was seated, he looked over to see I was still waiting. I waved at him and he waved back.

Then a little blond girl with pigtails sitting next to him leaned over and said something. He chuckled and then covered his mouth with his hand. I slipped away when I saw him relax a little. He was going to be okay.

He was a tough little cookie.

I only hoped I could do right by him.

Outside, I hopped onto one of the automated trolleys that were built to help the population get around the city dome. With everything as crowded as it was and with space at a premium, public transportation was a necessity.

I looked up at the large hexagonal sections of the dome above, the clear blue of the sky bright even through the panels. The sun was beating down like it usually was, but the dome was doing its job and buffering us against the harsh rays, making them gentle and human-friendly while also creating an environment where the atmosphere and air quality could be controlled.

Humans couldn't last long outside the dome. With the ozone as depleted as it was and the caustic chemicals polluting the air, it was so unfriendly that the domes had to be built, creating pockets of safety for the most-vulnerable race. With humans mostly confined to the city domes, dragons and phoenixes thrived in their own communities in the harsh environment outside, their hardier natures and affinity for the sun meaning they didn't have the same limitations.

When I'd first met Omari, he was a job. A job I was coerced into. I had a rule—I only handled inanimate objects, but he was still a job. He was part phoenix and sun-sick from lack of radiation exposure inside the dome. I thought I'd drop him off with his family in the phoenix territory, and that would be that.

Finding out that the whole thing had been a ploy to get me into phoenix territory was a surprise, to say the least. Discovering that the Phoenix King was my father and Omari was my brother hadn't even been on my radar.

After I found out Omari didn't have any real family to go back to—as far as I was concerned, King Emberich was nothing but a sperm donor for both of us—I'd thought long and hard about what to do. There was no question that he was staying with me. But could I come back to the city dome with him?

I knew it wasn't easy living here, having grown up around humans when I was part dragon and part phoenix—another surprise for me. My mother had been part dragon but had never revealed who dear old dad was. I would never have found out if Emberich hadn't concocted that plan to get me to his territory.

Why exactly, I didn't know. Though according to my newfound grandmother, it wasn't for any good reason. He was jealous of his power and what he perceived as any possible threat to it.

Great guy, right?

It was all still a trip. I was still getting used to having so much family now when I'd become accustomed to having none after my mother died.

As with most complicated things, my decision ultimately came down to a very practical issue. My work was in the city dome. The courier business that I'd built through pure hard work. My home, my life. Everything was here.

Ashur, Dragon Lord of the nearby dragon skein and my new...something...had wanted me and Omari to stay with him. I'd been tempted. But what if things didn't work out between us? I wouldn't be just putting my own life at risk, but also Omari's.

I needed to provide some kind of stability, or the closest I could get to it anyway. So I'd brought Omari back here. And I was determined to give him a good life. Which meant I'd have to work extra hard to make sure any lean times didn't affect him.

I adjusted the package under my arm. Starting with the first job today, I'd make this work for Omari's sake.

I got off the trolley about a block away from where my office was located. It wasn't the best area and it wasn't the worst. I didn't want to cut down on my potential client pool from the get-go with a place that discouraged either end of the income scale too much. From the street, the gray-brick structure with the short stoop looked pretty bland and innocuous, which I liked. I didn't want anything too eye- or attention-catching. The dentist on one side and the consignment shop on the other added to the mediocrity of the place.

I hopped up the short flight of stairs, opened the door, and entered the foyer. Generic flooring and lighting and a standard staircase that led up to the other businesses were the only things inside. I turned to the left, where the door with the frosted glass and my name in gold lettering was located.

I used the retinal scanner to get in, even though I didn't have much faith in it after the office had been broken into so easily by Santiago, the client I later realized was working for my father. But I hadn't changed anything. No security was really a hundred percent secure. Not if someone really wanted to get in. The retinal scanner kept my stuff from being stolen, which was all I really needed. I kept items to deliver on my person for the most part.

My office wasn't much to look at. One room, furnished, with a desk that had seen a lot of use, a wheeled chair for me, two chairs for potential clients, and cabinets against one wall that contained all the tools of the trade I'd accumulated thus far. Clothes, makeup, handcuffs.

Sometimes I got specific instructions on how to deliver something, like a birthday party last year that had required me to wear an evening gown. Not my favorite thing to do but now I had that gown tucked away in case something like that popped up again. The only art was one ambiguous painting of what I think was a bird hung on the wall opposite my desk. That was all I'd done in terms of decoration. I didn't have a large enough profit margin to add any more.

I logged into my computer to check emails, one of the least glamorous things about having my own business. Though still preferable to doing taxes. I scrolled through the potential clients, bills, and people trying to sell me stuff. I stopped at one that I didn't immediately recognize. The sender wasn't named. It was blocked out.

Highly illegal.

I clicked to open it. It was just one line, no greeting or signature.

Watch your back.

Huh.

I leaned back in my chair and considered it. My first

thought was that it was a threat. I'd worked for and with more than a few questionable characters. As long as I was paid, I didn't care. For the most part, they didn't mess with me and all I needed to do was get something from Point A to Point B, so I was willing to take those jobs after a little due diligence. But sometimes things didn't go exactly as planned.

When you worked with shady characters, life didn't always go smoothly. There were some not so great people out there who might not exactly love me. Though those people usually got only what was coming to them. I couldn't regret it—a lot of the time, the problem had to do with settling my bill. If I had to twist a few arms to be properly compensated, so be it.

On more rare occasions, the disagreement was about my life. They wanted to take it and I wasn't really okay with that. Go figure.

I tapped a finger on my desk as I stared at the line. Bottom line was, I couldn't really do anything about it. I could try to trace it back to the sender, but if they were able to send something without the identifier attached, then I doubted I'd find anything. They were too tech savvy.

So.

I'd be careful, like I always was. And I'd deal with whatever was thrown at me when and if it was. Shutting the computer down, I grabbed the package and stood up.

I had work to do.

ABOUT THE AUTHOR

USA Today Bestselling Author of fantasy and scifi romance, Miranda Martin's books feature larger than life heroes with out-of-this-world anatomy and smart heroines destined to save the world. As a little girl she would sneak off with her nose in a book, dreaming of magical realms. Today she brings those fantasies to life and adores every fan who chooses to live in them for a while.

She was born and raised in southern Virginia, but as a veteran she's traveled to places like Korea, Hawaii and good 'ole Texas. Now she's settled in Kansas, the heart of America, with her husband and daughters. Her favorite animals are dragons, unicorns and cats. If she's not writing, you can still find her tucked away somewhere with a warm blanket and her nose in a book.

Get in touch!
mirandamartinromance.com
miranda@mirandamartinromance.com

facebook.com/authormirandamartin
twitter.com/imMirandaMartin
instagram.com/imMirandaMartin